THE LAST GREAT SNAKE SHOW

ALSO BY TIM McLAURIN

The Acorn Plan

Woodrow's Trumpet

Keeper of the Moon: A Southern Boyhood

Cured by Fire

THE
LAST
GREAT
SNAKE
SHOW

TIM McLAURIN

G. P. Putnam's Sons ☆ *New York*

Copyright © 1997 by Tim McLaurin
*All rights reserved. This book, or parts thereof,
may not be reprinted in any form without permission.*

Published by G. P. Putnam's Sons
Publishers Since 1838
a member of
Penguin Putnam Inc.
200 Madison Avenue
New York, NY 10016

Published simultaneously in Canada

The text of this book is set in Fournier.
Book design by Marysarah Quinn

Library of Congress Cataloging-in-Publication Data

McLaurin, Tim.
The last great snake show / Tim McLaurin.
p.   cm.
ISBN 0-399-14280-0
I. Title.
PS3563.C3843L37   1997   97-9565 CIP
813'.54—dc21

Printed in the United States of America
1   3   5   7   9   10   8   6   4   2

This book is printed on acid-free paper. ∞

The writing of this novel has been like the tale that follows—a journey of discovery, famine and feast. I thank Rhoda Weyr for jump-starting the project; Anna Jardine for helping steer it along; Sue Reinhardt for offering low rent, friendship, and free advice; Bob Smith for keeping my ancient computer going; Sandy Arnold for nourishing my heart; and Faith Sale, my editor and friend, who always, somewhere down the line, makes me understand what the story is all about.

This book is dedicated to
Christopher Early McLaurin, my son.

If I might ask greatly of God,
my gift would be that one day hence,
you sit with your child upon your lap and say,
"I love you, as I know I am loved. We are the same
in flesh, blood, and soul."

I am south of equal
Under the north
The crumb beneath the crust
I rise slowly
In a land called an oven
Cheap white bread
Browning in criticism

Stirred up
By my beaten history
Jarred
By the cant of new judges
Who measure me
Incorrectly

I sweat hard
To gain respect
I sweep the old war
Out the door
And hold up a mirror
To insults

Sandy Arnold,
"War Wounds"

THE LAST GREAT SNAKE SHOW

Like a great serpent, the caravan of cars on the hill boiled up dust that was swept away by the sea breeze. Night had fallen, and The House of Joy was lit outside with neon like a carnival. The windows glowed with a softer tint from the party room, which was illuminated with oil lamps on the tables and black lights above the stage. Inside the house, the air smelled of fried seafood and hush puppies. Darlene Murphy stood at the front door and watched the guests arrive. She swept back a strand of hair.

"They're here," she shouted. "Man the battle stations."

A dozen people began to move. Clinton Tucker, dressed in a Confederate general's uniform, walked through the doorway, passing Darlene. She goosed him. The aged retired Army captain whirled around.

"God damn it, Darlene. Quit it. Bad enough me dressed up like a damn fool without you poking me in the ass."

"It's because you're so cute, Cap. Hey, look at all those dollar bills driving up here."

"Bunch of perverts. Wouldn't a one of them take up an air rifle if the goddamn Red China army marched in. Queers and sissies, high on dope . . ." His voice trailed off as he proceeded down the walkway to his post.

In the spacious barroom, the tables were topped with lacy cloths and magnolia blossoms arranged around kerosene lamps. Darlene and her girls, in low-cut antebellum dresses, stood ready at the tables. In one corner of the room, a four-man blues band tuned up.

The first car, a Lexus, entered the parking lot, followed by a Mercedes coupe and several other expensive models. A long black limousine brought up the rear. Cappy threw out his right arm and bent his elbow, then smartly touched his hat brim in salute.

"Hit it, Earl," Darlene instructed the man at the keyboard, who served as emcee.

"Yan-kees, fuck Yankees!" On the count, the band launched into a rousing rendition of "Dixie." The music spilled through the doorway and out into summer air. Darlene flashed a wide smile.

Men and women emerged from the vehicles, some in jeans and loafers, others in long dresses and tailored suits. A man slowly got out of the limousine. He was Jasper Dupree, a producer shooting his fourth movie in Wilmington, North Carolina, and a regular at Darlene's place. He extended his arm to a giggling young blonde in a halter top and spandex miniskirt.

Jasper sniffed the air. "Honey chil', you be in de Southland now," he said.

The guests moved up the lighted walkway past Cappy, some greeting him, others staring with either amusement or amazement. When Jasper and the woman reached Cappy, Jasper threw his own arm up in an exaggerated salute.

"Evening, General."

"Good evening, sir."

"You have a party planned for us tonight?"

"Sir, we're gonna make Mardi Gras look like a debutante ball."

"Gooood!"

"What's a debutante ball?" the woman asked.

"It's another one of those southern things." From his shirt pocket, Jasper took out a roll of money, then handed Cappy a hundred-dollar bill. "Carry on, General," he said.

Cappy nodded. He folded down the fingers on either side of his middle finger on his salute hand.

"Mighty glad to have y'all," Darlene said as the guests passed her at the front door. "We're real pleased to have you visit." People seated themselves at the tables, Jasper and the blonde and select guests taking the one nearest the stage. Darlene recognized a few faces from movies she had seen. Cappy came and stood beside her; he would be sergeant at arms and control the bar lights.

"Looks like we have a class act tonight." Cappy whistled. "Ol' Jasper slid me a hundred walking in."

"Who's that guy next to him?" Darlene asked. "What movie was he in?"

"I don't watch movies," Cappy said.

When the last chair had been scraped across the floor, Darlene held up a crystal bell and tinkled it until the crowd quieted. "We're plumb tickled to have y'all here with us tonight. We plan to show y'all southern hospitality at its best. You want anything not on the menu"—Darlene paused and winked—"all you need to do is ask."

"Hell, yeah!" Jasper shouted. Catcalls went up from several of the tables. The band started "The Battle of New Orleans," and the waitresses handed out menus. At the beginning of the second verse,

Cappy switched on a spotlight above the stage. From behind the curtain stepped Gloria Peacock, a Confederate flag draped around her. The crowd erupted into hoots.

"Introducing Glo-ri-a," Earl shouted into the mike. "Her great-great-grandma worked in chains, and let's just say, it's become a fam-i-ly tradition."

"The blacker the berry, the sweeter the juice," Jasper yelled.

Slowly, Glory let the flag slip down her shoulders into a pile on the floor. Her dark skin had been oiled, and in the spotlight it gleamed. Around her neck and belly were dozens of thin gold chains; besides that she wore only gold pasties and a braided gold G-string. She undulated with such energy that by the end of the song, perspiration beaded her skin.

Jasper moved his eyes from Glory's gyrations to the menu. "You've got to try the frog legs, Kelli," he told the blonde woman.

"I am *not* eating a frog!"

"Try it, baby. Tastes just like chicken."

"Then I'll eat chicken."

"They don't serve chicken."

Jasper stood. "Miss Darlene. I'd like to order a round of dew for the house."

Indeed, The House of Joy did not serve chicken. Depending on the season and what Cappy and Jubal caught, the menu varied: boiled peel-and-eat shrimp, fried catfish or flounder, steamed oysters or clams, bullfrog legs, venison steaks, and occasionally something like snapping turtle soup or baked raccoon. Small, crisp hush puppies with onion bits were a house specialty, as were cole slaw and collard greens. But anyone looking for a baked potato and steak, or a garden salad, was in the wrong place. Down-home southern was what the guests wanted, and that's what they got.

The beverage list ranged from cold Budweiser to the best brands of bourbon. For those customers who were known by face—and who asked—high-quality corn liquor could be purchased by the shot glass or by the gallon jug to go. The moonshine was made by one of Cappy's friends, who watered the brew down to about a hundred proof.

The band started into "Honky Tonk Women" next. The waitresses marched from the kitchen with trays holding shot glasses, lime wedges, and pint jars filled with cold moonshine. Jasper immediately poured himself two shots and knocked them back, then bit into a lime.

"Fire up!" he shouted, blinking back tears. "Fire up, you bunch of moviemaking motherfuckers."

Glory was glistening with sweat by the time the tables had been served their moonshine. Another song was beginning when Jasper raised his hand with a twenty-dollar bill. As fluid as water, Glory thrust out her long leg and stepped from the stage onto the middle of his table. She stood above him, smiling down as she moved. Jasper folded the bill lengthwise, then stuck one end between his teeth. Glory gyrated lower and lower until she was on her knees, her pelvis only inches from Jasper's face. She bent forward until her breasts were even with his eyes. Jasper leaned forward; Glory cupped his face with her bosom, pushed her breasts together like twin pillows, and gradually withdrew. Staring into his eyes, she licked her lips, then took the bill from his mouth between her own teeth and sprang upright. She slipped the twenty into her G-string.

"Hot damn almighty!" Jasper shouted. Kelli's eyes and mouth were wide open. Bills appeared in the mouths of two other men.

At The House of Joy, any activities beyond table dances were between Glory and the other girls, and their customers. Darlene looked the other way, so that if and when the sheriff, whom she had known for years, stopped by, she could say she kept the dancing legal. Darlene did have a cookie jar in the kitchen where the women could contribute twenty-five percent of any profits to the house if they got lucky. The jar was never empty.

IN A SPARE BEDROOM in the rear of the house, Jubal Lee undressed. Six-foot-two, with sandy hair and blue eyes, he was lean and tanned from hours spent searching the swampland. He slipped out of his jeans and pulled on a Tarzan-style loincloth.

In a plastic bucket on the bed, sounding like a swarm of bees, was coiled a five-foot-long canebrake rattler.

"Hold your horses," Jubal addressed the snake. "Wait till this set is finished, and you'll get your chance. I want you rattling then, buzzing like a chain saw."

Jubal ran his fingers through his hair to muss it as the last song of the set began. He took a deep breath and examined himself in the mirror, ignoring how silly he looked. He thought only of the money he would make. When he lifted the bucket and thumped the side, the rattler immediately started buzzing.

"Get mad, bad-ass. It's showtime."

When Glory finally came off the stage, the party had been going on for two hours. Every table in the barroom was strewn with shrimp shells, greasy plates, and beer bottles. Darlene had sold nearly a gallon of corn liquor. Three men had ventured into the back rooms for private attention. Cappy, still posted at the front door, was tipsy from his own shots of bourbon; Darlene was gabby and gay from a long day of sipping beer. The only sober head in the house was Jubal, who stood behind the curtain, waiting for Earl to call him in.

A drumroll sounded, and Earl began: "Ladies and gentlemen. For your private entertainment, The House of Joy tonight brings you exclusively an act of daring and bravery found only within the walls of this humble domain."

Jasper, who was now glassy-eyed, gripped Kelli's arm. "You gotta see this. This is un-fucking-real."

Kelli shook her head. "In this place, baby, everything is un-fucking-real." She slurred her words.

All the lights in the room except the table lanterns went out. A woman shrieked. The stage was black, and when the spotlight came on, Jubal could be seen on one knee, a coiled, rattling snake only a few feet away.

"Jesus!" Kelli said. "Is it real?"

"As real as sin," Jasper replied.

In what appeared a trance, Jubal concentrated on the snake's eyes. The rattler saw only one foe; it tightened closer into its coil and raised its head into the air. The rattle was a blur of motion, the warning heard clearly throughout the room.

"Introducing Jubal Lee," Earl shouted, "a southern son of the swampland. Aided only by his bare hands, he will attempt to capture this deadly poisonous rattlesnake. Don't blink, friends. He has the quickest hands south of the Mason-Dixon line."

"Jubilee," Kelli said. "What a beautiful name."

When Jubal leaned forward, the rattler raised its head higher and cocked its neck like a spring. Jubal reached with his left arm and held his hand in front of the serpent. He slowly wiggled his fingers to hold the snake's attention, while even more slowly shifting his weight to the right. He then brought his right arm in a wide arc behind the snake. When the snake shifted its attention from the decoy hand to Jubal's face, Jubal first froze, then wiggled his fingers faster.

The snake struck like a bolt of lightning. Jubal jerked backward; the fangs missed his hand by an inch. Several guests shrieked and gasped. Instantly, the serpent was back in its coil, rattle buzzing, ready to strike again. Jubal had to start over. Twice more the rattler struck, and each time Jubal jerked back just in time. Silence hung like wet cotton over the room, the only noise a nervous cough or the clink of a beer bottle. Darlene's face was creased with deep lines as she watched from the kitchen door.

Jubal moved in again. After a few minutes of torturously deliberate movement, his right hand was only six inches behind the rattler's neck. Even faster than the serpent could strike, Jubal's hand flashed and his fingers closed around the snake's thick neck, half an inch below the jaws. In that instant, the serpent's mouth gaped open, exposing fangs an inch long. The rattler bit into the air, squirting twin streams of venom that carried six feet. Jubal clasped his free hand around the snake's midsection, stood quickly, and lifted the beast over his head.

The audience was stunned into silence. Then Kelli jumped to her feet and started the place clapping, yelling, and stomping. Jubal walked to Jasper's table. He kneeled, released the snake's midsection, and reached for a shot glass. He raised the lip of the glass to the rattler's mouth. The snake bit down, fangs lapping over the edge of the vessel and squirting honey-colored venom. Out flowed a half-inch of poison. Jubal tipped his head back, poured the venom into his mouth and swallowed it. He sprang to his feet and disappeared behind the curtain as the audience screamed approval. After a few moments he reappeared, without the snake, and bowed.

Kelli stood in her chair, arms raised to the ceiling, a hundred-dollar bill in her mouth. Jubal walked to the edge of the stage and kneeled again. The woman pulled down the waistband of his loin-cloth and, using just her teeth, slipped the bill inside.

"Jubal Lee!" Earl shouted. "Fastest son of the South, live only at the one-and-only House of Joy."

Darlene walked between the tables, collecting tips for Jubal in her plumed hat. Kelli motioned for Jubal to lean closer. She kissed him hard on the lips until he pulled away. He flashed her a big, fake smile, then left through the curtain as the band began another set.

In his room, Jubal unscrewed a bottle of Listerine, and gargled the liquid deep in his throat—more to rid himself of any germs that blonde might have been carrying than to erase the taste of snake venom. He opened the window and spat through the screen, then breathed in great lungfuls of fragrant air.

THE PARTY WENT ON until one o'clock, when finally the band launched into "Last Call for Alcohol" and Darlene politely told the blonde woman she needed to put her halter top back on and get down from the stage. Jasper ordered a jug of moonshine to go. He studied the night's bill, counted out ten hundreds into a pile on the table, paused, then added two more hundreds.

"Wasn't this the goddamnedest thing you ever saw?" he said to

Kelli. He put one arm around her waist to support her. Her halter top was back on, but it was pulled down on one side, exposing her nipple.

"Jasper, I want the snake boy," she slurred. "Can I take him with me?"

Jasper guided her toward the entrance. "Let's go, babe. I got an anaconda waiting for you." He saluted Cappy at the door.

"FROM NOW ON, you leave them big snakes in the woods," Darlene scolded Jubal. "That snake bit you, you'd be dead right now."

It was nearly three, and Jubal, Cappy, and Darlene were cleaning the last of the mess in the bar.

"Snake's never going to bite me," Jubal defended himself. "I won't let it."

"A small rattler will be just as impressive as a big one," Darlene continued. "Most of those people have never even seen a live rattler. I was scared to death when you were up there tonight."

"You saw what that woman gave me. I never used such a big rattler before, and I never got tipped a hundred-dollar bill before."

Cappy snorted. "Shit. That hundred dollars was like a quarter to that woman. She woulda tried to buy you if you hadn't gotten out of there." He shook his head. "These customers are getting stranger all the time. Perverted. Damn country is getting like Rome before the fall."

"But we're making money like all get-out," Darlene said. "Dennis Hopper is starting a new film next month. You remember what his crowd is like!"

"I better start to bed," Cappy told her. "Got to net them shrimp tomorrow. Feed the perverted masses."

Darlene reached and touched his arm. "It's so late. Why don't you stay with me?"

"Then I wouldn't get one second of sleep."

Darlene winked at Jubal. "What's getting wrong with you, Cap? All them push-ups making your dick limp? It's getting to where I have to bribe you into bed."

"You ought to stay, Cappy." Jubal joined the fun. "There's a full moon tonight. Might be a werewolf outside."

Cappy frowned at Jubal. He nodded toward Darlene. "Would you fuck that?"

Jubal opened his mouth, then closed it. He blushed.

"Come on," Cappy demanded. "Don't go mute on me now." He leaned toward Jubal and lowered his voice. "Would you fuck it?"

Jubal was suddenly in a hurry. "I need to go. I'll see y'all tomorrow."

"Better watch out for that werewolf," Cappy said.

Jubal could hear Cappy laughing as he walked out the back door and into the heavy July night.

THE BACKBONE of the Great Smokies rolled against the weak light of the western sky, the peaks muted by a soft drizzle. Jubal stood on a rocky outcrop, gazing toward the mountains. Below him, the earth dropped a sheer hundred feet into a gorge, where an invisible waterfall murmured a song about time and rocks.

Jubal's gaze moved from left to right, following the blade of the peaks. He wished that he and his companions were already days and miles beyond the Continental Divide. He imagined his feet planted in sand where the ocean met the land and the sun buried herself in the sea instead of in great piles of rock. Maybe then, when there was no more path for fleeing on, he would be forced to turn and try to understand why he had fled.

Life had changed like the sudden streak of a meteor. The mountains comfortably shrouded in mist contrasted with the chaos of the previous two weeks. One tornado, and The House of Joy had been leveled to the basement, and Miss Darlene left with a splinter of glass embedded inoperably in her brain. And now here they were, nearly broke, taking the show on the road, in order to fulfill Darlene's last wish—to return to the coastland of Oregon, where she was born.

"Hey, Cappy," Jubal said over his shoulder to the aging man swearing under his breath as he tried to suspend a tarpaulin from some trees. "Come up here and look at this view. You can see forever."

"I ain't ready to see eternity yet," Cappy replied, blowing out a stream of cigarette smoke with his words. "Right now I need to get this canvas up before the bottom falls out of the sky. I could use some help." He cocked one hand on his hip, his forearm covered with faded green and black tattoos.

Jubal turned his back to the deepening twilight and scanned the campsite. Before a backdrop of spruce trees sat an old school bus. It had once been owned by a gospel group, and the original paint had faded to a Carolina blue, but the words "Jubilee Express" were still clearly stenciled in white on the sides. The luggage rack on top was piled high with rolls of white canvas, beams of lumber, coils of electrical wire, and a large tool chest.

A buxom black woman in her early thirties sat at a picnic table beneath the drooping canvas. In front of her, over a camping stove, a frying pan sizzled with hot grease. The woman fanned at the smoke rising from the pan. Jubal walked to the table, grasped a corner of the tarp, and stretched it to the nearest tree, where he threaded a cord through a grommet and tied it around a branch above his head.

"Those hot dogs are smelling good, Glory," he said. "I could eat a dozen."

"Well, three's your limit, if everyone gets equal," she answered. "That is, if the damn bugs and skitters don't get 'em first."

Insects darted in and out of the glow of a gasoline lantern. Cappy tied off the last corner of the tarp, then lifted the center of the canvas with a sapling he had cut down. "Unless a monsoon sets in, we ought to eat dry." He straightened the sapling and nudged the bottom with the toe of his boot. "You want to help me get Darlene out here?" he said to Glory.

She stepped back from the stove and handed Jubal a fork. "Don't let 'em burn. That can of pork and beans can go in next."

"I can't cook," Jubal protested. "What if I burn my hand? We'll be up the creek then."

"And what if I burn my ass? We'll be up the creek without a paddle."

"Y'all quit fussing," Cappy said. "We have enough trouble without you two going at each other."

Jubal turned the hot dogs, and slid the burning ones in the middle to the edges of the pan. When they seemed ready, he forked the hot dogs and put them on a paper plate. He opened a can of beans, turned it upside down over the greasy pan. A cloud of smoke rose; the grease spit and burned the back of his left hand. "Dammit!" Jubal sucked at the wound.

From the door of the bus, Darlene emerged, held on either side by Cappy and Glory. She was still weak and pale from her time in the hospital; a square gauze bandage covered the wound in her forehead. She paused once to gain her balance, then reached up and removed the hands supporting her.

"I ain't an invalid," she said.

"We just don't want you to fall, Miss Darlene," Glory said.

"I could walk a strand of barbed wire right now," Darlene answered. Slowly but steadily, she walked the few yards to the picnic table and sat down on the edge of the bench. "Those hot dogs smell like the Fourth of July." Even now, in her early sixties, she was a beautiful woman, with thick black hair streaked with silver, high cheekbones, and eyes like a clear winter sky. She took a deep breath. "I always loved mountain air."

Jubal turned off the gas to the burner. "Chow's on."

"We ought to say the blessing first," Glory said.

"Since when did you get so religious?" Jubal asked.

"I always been spiritual. Especially since that tornado nearly sucked me into the sky. I'm even official. Got a mail-order ordination from a Bible college."

"Yeah, I bet."

"I can prove it, Mr. Smarty-Pants."

"Stop arguing," Darlene said. "Glory's right. We have a lot to be thankful for."

The four lowered their heads while Glory said a blessing. When she had finished, Jubal excused himself to get some lawn chairs from the storage hold; Darlene might feel more comfortable sitting on one.

He took a flashlight from the dashboard of the bus and went to the rear, where he lifted the creaky luggage door of the storage compartment. "You fellows all right?" Jubal whispered. From inside one of the wooden boxes issued the soft whirr of rattlesnakes. Jubal thumped the side of the box. The snakes buzzed louder. "How was the ride? You fellows hang tight. You can get your fifteen minutes of fame, and I'll set you free."

The snakes' warnings were joined by a long, low moan. Jubal listened closer. He heard the moan again, then the sound of something moving. Shining the light deeper into the hold, Jubal saw the mound of the folded carnival tent, then tennis shoes protruding below the canvas. Startled, he paused a moment, then climbed on top of the boxes of angry snakes. He sucked in his breath as he shone the light up the body of a slender young woman lying on her back, arms limp by her sides, face turned away from him. Her chest rose and fell slowly.

"Hey, Cap," Jubal shouted. "Come here."

At the sound of Jubal's voice, the woman raised one arm.

"What is it?" Cappy answered.

"It's trouble," Jubal yelled.

"LORD, she's just a child." Darlene stroked the young woman's cheek. "Can't be much more than twenty."

"What she doing in the bottom of that bus?" Glory asked. "Laying in there with them damn snakes."

Once he and Cappy had pulled the young woman from the hold, Jubal hoisted her into his arms and carried her to his mattress in the bus. Darlene put a wet cloth across her forehead. The woman kept mumbling and trying to sit up.

"Lay there, honey," Darlene said. "We're not going to hurt you. You lay still."

"Maybe we ought to take her clothes off," Cappy suggested.

"Now you the sick one," Glory said.

"Hell, maybe she got bit by one of those rattlers," Cappy exclaimed. "I ain't wanting to see her damn tits!"

"What do you think, Jubal?" Darlene asked. "You been mighty quiet."

"The snake cages are all locked up. I think it was the fumes. She was lying right above the tailpipe. She could have died."

"Maybe we ought to call an ambulance," Glory said.

Darlene removed the cloth from the woman's forehead, wet it again in cold water, then put it back. "Her color is getting better. I think she's all right. But how in the world did she get down there?"

"God almighty," Cappy said. "This is all we need. A fugitive."

"Hush," Darlene told him. "She ain't a fugitive. Look at her hands, her nails. She doesn't exactly look like a gun moll."

"She looks like a pack of trouble to me."

The young woman moaned again. Her eyelids fluttered, then opened. She stared flatly toward the ceiling; suddenly her eyes cleared and she sat up and looked wildly around the bus. "Goodness. Where am I?"

Darlene placed her hand on the young woman's shoulder. "Easy, honey. You're all right."

"Where am I?" Her eyes stopped at Jubal's face.

He crouched on one knee and extended his hand. "I'm Jubal. What's your name?"

The woman opened her mouth, and her eyes shifted to her lap, then back to Jubal. "I'm Kitty. Kitty Buckstar."

"Fancy name," Glory said. "Sounds like a country music singer."

"How'd you get in the bus?" Jubal asked.

Kitty swallowed and stared at her hands. "I was robbed." She looked at Jubal. "Yes, two men grabbed my purse and robbed me. I ran and they chased me. I hid in your bus at a gas station."

Cappy narrowed one eye and looked at Darlene. "You didn't know these men?" he asked.

Kitty shook her head. "I was frightened and ran. I thought they would hurt me."

"Where are you from, honey?" Darlene asked.

"Wilmington."

"Where is your family?"

"I don't have any."

"You have any ID, Miss?" Cappy asked.

"I don't even have my wallet. They took it."

Cappy snorted. He turned and walked to the cooler and took out a beer.

"You hungry?" Jubal asked.

Kitty nodded.

"I'll get you a plate of hot dogs and beans."

While Kitty ate, Jubal and the others stood outside in the glow of the lamp, talking softly.

"She's lying," Cappy said. "She wasn't robbed."

"We don't know that," Jubal said.

"I know it, and Darlene knows it. We weren't born yesterday."

"She's hiding something, all right," Darlene said. "But I think she's harmless. Probably a runaway."

"Probably a rich runaway," Glory said. "You see her skin? Looks like she bathes in Oil of Olay."

"So what do we do with her?" Cappy asked. "She can't stay with us. We have enough mouths to feed."

"She can stay the night," Darlene said. "We can't just turn her out."

"She can have my mattress," Jubal said.

"Without you in it. You got to keep your mind on the business ahead." Glory stared at the petite young woman, whose skin was as white and flawless as whole milk.

THE SMELL OF FRYING BACON wafted through the air, mixed with the odor of coffee. The sun had not crested the mountains yet and the campground was in shadows; doves called their sad notes from the pine tops. Kitty had awakened with a start and looked about wildly before her memory kicked in. Except for a dull headache, she felt pretty good despite the adventure she'd had the day before. Last night, she remembered, she had eaten a slightly burned hot dog and a plate of beans; then the older woman had given her a pill and said she should get some sleep. She had slept inside a sleeping bag on a mattress, the black woman on one side of her, the old man on the other. The young man had disappeared outside.

Now she was alone in the bus, wondering what she should do next. She felt her jeans pocket, where she had stashed fifteen hundred dollars in big bills. She had a tote bag with a few changes of clothes, but not her purse with her airline ticket and driver's license and credit cards, no legal thread remaining to the life she had lived for nearly twenty-one years.

From outside the bus, she could hear low voices. The smell of coffee made her realize she was actually hungry in the morning, for the first time in ages. The pill she had taken seemed to have cleared her blood; her memories of pills and what they did to people were still too vivid—all the Valium and other things she had watched her mother take over the years. She recalled Cornelia Monroe and the life that she, as Kitty, had fled.

MORNING ILLUMINATED the closed curtains in Cornelia's bedroom. She lay under the covers in fetal position, wishing she could fall into deep sleep, but the real world was calling.

She heard the door open, then the sound of feet on the carpet. She felt a hand on her shoulder.

"Baby, you got to wake up. It's nine-thirty and your mama is in a tizzy downstairs."

"I don't want to wake up," Cornelia mumbled.

Esther pulled the covers down to Cornelia's shoulders. She sat down on the edge of the bed and rubbed the young woman's back. "What's the matter, honey? You ought to be up at the crack of day. You done graduated—got a college degree. Victor will be here in an hour to pick you up for the brunch. Get on up now."

Esther walked to the window and pulled the curtains open, letting the room fill with the bright June day. "See what a pretty morning you missing."

Cornelia sat up blinking. "I don't want to go to another brunch. This is the second brunch. There have been three dinner parties already, and the wedding is still a week away. I'm sick of it."

"You're a popular girl," Esther said, turning to face Cornelia. Esther was close to sixty, a slender woman of mixed blood who had worked for the family since Cornelia was a baby. "A lot of girls would love to trade places with you."

"I'd like to trade places with a lot of them."

Esther planted one hand on her hip. "How can you say that? You got a handsome husband-to-be. You gonna have the biggest wedding ever been in Wilmington. Then you going to fly off to Paris for two weeks. I never been to Paris."

"I've been twice already. I'd rather go to the Rocky Mountains."

Esther sat in a chair by the window. "Cornelia. You want to get married, don't you? You did say yes to Victor's proposal."

"I said yes."

"Then why aren't you happy?"

Cornelia lifted her head and stared at Esther. "Would you be happy with Victor? Your husband hugs and kisses you every evening when he picks you up to go home, and you've been married for years and years. The only time Victor ever kisses me is when he wants something, and you know what that is."

"Cornelia!" Esther exclaimed. "Hush that sort of talk."

Cornelia put her hands to her face for a moment, then removed them. "I guess I love him. If I even know what love is."

"You'll know if it's real."

"That's what bothers me."

Esther stood up. "Now get dressed. Your mama is in a tizzy, I told you. She said to get you down there."

"I'll be down as soon as I shower."

Anna Belle, Cornelia's mother, and Frank, her stepfather, were sitting over coffee in the breakfast room when Cornelia came downstairs. She was in a sundress, her hair pinned up.

"Good morning," she said.

Frank nodded and continued reading the paper. Anna Belle looked at her daughter. "You took your time coming down, dear. Did you sleep well?"

Anna Belle came from a prominent Savannah family. She had married Cornelia's father, Will Monroe, against her family's wishes, swept off her feet by the rugged, handsome fisherman with big dreams. Before Cornelia's birth, he left the fishing industry and became a realtor, and by the time of his unexpected death he had amassed a small fortune in the coastal development boom. Only a year after he died, Anna Belle married Frank, a distant cousin of Will's, who was even more shrewd in business than Will had been. The Monroe name was one of the best known in Wilmington.

Cornelia took a seat and Esther poured her a cup of coffee. "You want a danish, honey?" Esther asked.

Cornelia shook her head.

"Drink your coffee," Anna Belle said. "We have a dozen things to do today, and you sleeping all morning hasn't helped."

"Mother, we were at the party until one last night."

"I was up early. Frank was up early. Victor called at nine, and you were still in bed."

"I'm tired."

"And I'm tired of you moping around here. You're a grown woman, Cornelia. I've put a lot of money and tremendous energy into this wedding, and I expect a little appreciation."

"Yes ma'am."

The phone rang, and Esther hurried to answer it. She spoke, then took the phone from her ear. "It's the newspaper calling, Miz Monroe."

"Hand it here. Took them long enough to return my call." Anna Belle put the receiver to her ear. "Yes, Martha. . . . Thank you for calling. . . . Yes, Cornelia is fine. . . . What I was calling about is, I want your assurance that the wedding announcement will top the page. You know we've contributed quite a bit of money in advertisements. I know the paper would hate to lose that support. . . ."

KITTY STRAINED to understand the voices, but they were too
distant. She didn't know anything about these people. She could tell
the older man and woman were suspicious of her. She wasn't even
sure where the group was going. But from the way the bus had been
outfitted like a camper, she reasoned they planned to stay on the
road for a while. They didn't seem dangerous. They were going
west. Maybe they would let her ride with them for the day, or drop
her at the next airport. She wondered whether she'd be able to buy
another plane ticket without an ID.

Her original plan had been to fly to Jackson Hole and hide out in
a hotel at the edge of the Tetons. Mountains were opaque, a contrast
to the translucent Carolina waters. Her mother and stepfather and
fiancé would never find her in Wyoming, and maybe then, beneath
the shadows of rock, she would begin to find her own form.

But the plane ticket she'd bought was gone, and lying there
wouldn't solve anything. Kitty wiggled out of the sleeping bag and
walked to the door of the bus.

They were all sitting at the picnic table. Four faces turned toward her.

"Morning," Jubal said. "I was fixing to wake you up."

"Good morning," Kitty responded.

"You sleep good, honey?" Glory said. "I hope there wasn't a
pea under your mattress."

"Oh, I slept like a log. That pill really worked."

"Well, come on over here, Kitty, and eat some breakfast," Darlene said. "We just sat down."

"Thank you. I hope I'm not a bother. I know I wasn't expected."

Kitty sat at the end of the bench beside Glory. An iron skillet held scrambled eggs, and a paper plate strips of bacon. "This smells wonderful," Kitty said.

Jubal lifted the coffeepot, filled a styrofoam cup, and handed it to her.

"Thank you." Kitty noticed the old woman searching her face. She also noticed the bandage in the middle of the woman's forehead. She blinked and looked down at her coffee.

"You said you were robbed yesterday?" Cappy asked.

"Yes sir."

"Don't call me sir. My name is Clinton. You can call me Cappy if you like. Do you know who robbed you?"

Kitty felt the blood rising in her face. She took a slow breath. "I was waiting for a taxi to the airport. Two men came up to me and grabbed my purse. When I ran, they chased me. One of them had a knife."

Cappy glanced at Darlene, then looked back at Kitty. "Where are you from, if you don't mind telling," he said.

Kitty took another slow breath. She told them how she'd grown up in a Baptist children's home in Wilmington, how she'd left the home at eighteen and been on her own for two years. "I was on my way to Wyoming to start a new life when those men robbed me. Now I don't know what I'm going to do."

"You poor thing," Glory said.

"If you could drop me near an airport, I would appreciate it."

"We're heading west," Jubal said. "You're welcome to ride. But we ain't as fast as no airplane."

★ 25 ★

"Wait a minute," Cappy said.

"We need a cook," Jubal insisted. "I can't risk burning my hand."

"Wait a goddamn minute." Cappy stood. "Miss, would you mind taking a short hike. Me and my colleagues need to have a little discussion."

"Oh, certainly." Kitty set her coffee down. "I need to go to the ladies' room, anyway. I guess there is one?"

"There's a privy straight down that path." Cappy pointed, then watched Kitty's back until she was beyond earshot. "Look, y'all," he began. "We don't need that girl riding with us. We've barely got the money to feed ourselves. We don't know who the hell she is, or where she's been."

"I burn a lot of calories on that stage," Glory said. "Hot dogs ain't gonna cut it for long."

"She doesn't look like she eats too much," Jubal said. "She ain't big as a minute. Maybe she could help drive the bus too."

"Aw, shit," Cappy answered.

Darlene stiffened in her seat. She lifted her hand and pressed her fingertips to the bandage.

"You all right?" Cappy asked.

Darlene was silent for a few seconds. When she started speaking her words were slow. "The rocks are black and wet along the shoreline. Don't step that way. Turn to the east if you must jump. The water is deep there. You can save her."

Cappy squinted and furrowed his brow. "What in the hell you talking about?"

Darlene lowered her hands slowly.

"You all right, Miss Darlene?" Glory asked. "Do you need to lay down?"

Darlene shook her head. She stared into Cappy's eyes. "Captain. The girl is going with us."

DARLENE LAY in the rear of the bus, which had been partitioned with boards and drapes to make a bedroom for her. The throbbing in her head eased only after she lay quietly for several minutes with her eyes closed. At the picnic table, she had seen the black rocks and foaming sea clearly. She had dreamed of the same rocks and water a few nights earlier.

The doctors who had examined Darlene after the tornado had not been optimistic. If she were to have an operation to remove the glass embedded in her brain, there was a fifty-fifty chance she'd be left a vegetable. Without the operation, though, the glass might soon cause blindness, then a fatal hemorrhage.

Darlene touched the bandage over the wound. A tingle like a light charge of electricity pierced her head. At night, strange dreams filled her sleep; when she was awake, images popped into her mind, people and objects, dim and unfocused. When she was in the hospital, she knew who was coming through the door before they even knocked, as if the glass had tuned her to a higher frequency.

When she heard the bus engine roar into power, Darlene felt no fear of death, no fear of the miles before her. For twenty years she had made the payments on five acres of land on the Oregon coastline, and just as she knew she had lived a full and good life, she also knew she would return to her land and breathe in the smell of junipers and salt air.

I CAN'T BELIEVE I'm going home. All these years living the width of the continent away from where I was born. And now I'll be buried there—probably sooner than later—but at least I'll be in the dirt of my roots.

Sitting in this bed, I feel the South receding from me, the memory like a warm glow on my back. I was never really a total part of that culture. I tried to be. I adapted my speech and my food, but I was never of the born-and-bred. I don't know if a person can truly ever leave her heritage behind, erase it like a blackboard. She carries some of it with her, and tries to change the new land to mirror where she came from.

As I know I am dying, the old South is dying too. Oh, how much Wilmington has changed in twenty years. It hardly resembles the small port town where I opened my first bar. The streets are now boulevards, the marshes and forest cut and bulldozed to make room for subdivisions and strip malls. Most of the convenience stores are operated by Arabs and Palestinians who play music from their homelands while taking money for Marlboros and Budweiser.

But I can't blame them any more than I can Yankees or Californians for coming in and buying up land and building big houses, then complaining about the crowded roads and schools and the fact that most stores don't stock smoked salmon or imported beer. I came too, looking for the good life. I made my home with a people and a culture. I paid for land on a quiet, unspoiled coast where, when the streets elsewhere were too wide and the accents too mingled and tainted, I could escape.

At least I will admit to that.

FORTUNATELY, Kitty remembered from driver's education how to work a clutch. With Jubal at her side, she stalled out only twice before she got the bus rolling. The vehicle lurched at first like a bounding rabbit. When she tried to change gears, it sounded like fingernails on a blackboard.

"You have to mash the clutch in all the way," Jubal shouted.

"My legs aren't long enough."

Jubal leaned and pulled a knob, and the seat leaped forward. Kitty shifted and the bus picked up speed down the gravel drive. By the time she had entered the ramp to the interstate, the drama had left Kitty's driving.

"You're a pro," Jubal told her.

"What's the speed limit?" she asked.

"You don't have to worry about that. This thing will barely do fifty-five. Just put the pedal to the metal and ride." He lifted a Rand McNally road atlas from the dash, then sat down beside Cappy.

Kitty stared at the splattered bugs on the windshield. She would have to remember to clean them off when they stopped for gas. Beyond them, the mountains were rapidly yielding to the rolling hills and meadows of eastern Tennessee; the countryside was green and pretty. Kitty kept her foot jammed against the gas pedal and tried not to listen to the voice inside her head.

My God, what am I doing? Am I crazy? I don't even know these people. Snakes, and God knows what kind of dancing they're talking about. That old woman keeps looking at me like she's staring into my soul. This bus might break down any second. I should get off in the next town and take a taxi to the closest airport. If I had any sense, I'd go back home.

Kitty thought of the money in her pocket. No way could she let these people know how much she had. That fifteen hundred dollars was her only security against a humiliating return home.

EARLIER THAT MORNING, she had tried to break away from the group. "If you'd just let me ride to the next town, I'd appreciate it," she had said.

"Ma'am, you're not wanted by the law, are you?" Cappy asked. "You're not in some kind of trouble?"

"Oh, no. Nothing like that."

"Do you have any money? I know it's none of my business, but we're on a tight budget here."

"I have some money. I had some credit cards in my purse, but they're gone now."

Cappy sighed. "We're not the kind of people to turn our back on someone in need. You can ride with us as far as you want. If you can help out with the work, we'd appreciate it."

"Oh, I'd be glad to help out. What sort of work?"

Glory threw back her head and laughed. "Child, you are in for some kinda education. Let me fill you in. You riding with the last of a breed. What we do has been going on since the Garden of Eden, but I believe that time is running out."

Kitty arched her eyebrows. "What exactly is it you do?"

Glory cackled again. "There was a house once—boy, was it a house—and it stood on a hill beside a river. The show we put on there, it would put Las Vegas to shame. I hardly know where to begin. . . ."

Kitty's eyes were filled with wonder after listening to Glory's description of The House of Joy. She had heard of such places, had even been in a class at Hollins with a girl who supposedly spent a summer dancing topless at a bar in Myrtle Beach.

Glory laughed at the expression on Kitty's face. "You don't have to worry, white girl. That stage belongs to Glory. There ain't no prejudice up there. Everybody's money is green."

THEY ATE LUNCH on the road: Vienna sausages and saltines covered with squirt cheese from a can. Kitty washed the food down with Pepsi straight from the bottle. The land steadily rolled by and flattened, the hills were left miles behind. When they stopped for gas, Kitty cleaned bugs off the windshield. She bought a postcard and a stamp, and went to the bathroom to write: "Dear Esther, if I never am heard from again, I want you to have this last note from me."

She slipped the postcard into a mailbox before boarding the bus. She would just have to hope Esther wouldn't tell anyone she'd heard from her.

Jubal took over the driving, so Kitty napped on a mattress; the drone of tires and wind was as soothing as a lullaby. When she woke up, the sun was low in the sky. She saw Cappy pointing at a road sign.

"It's the next exit," he said. "The town's about five miles north."

Jubal nodded and left the interstate. They were fifteen miles east of St. Louis. The land was flat and nearly treeless, and the skyline of the big city jutted from the horizon, the giant archway glinting like gold.

"Makes me want a cheeseburger," Cappy said.

"Who the hell does Jasper know in St. Louis?" Jubal asked. "I thought he was strictly California."

"He's strictly perverted," Cappy said. "There's a network of them all across the United States. We might as well be riding into Sodom right now."

"They can be perverted long as they like," Glory said. "Just so they got the cold cash to back it up. I like it a little strange, anyhow."

Kitty left the mattress and took a seat beside Glory. "Where are we?"

"A few minutes from the gates of hell," Cappy answered.

Jubal laughed.

"What do you mean?"

"Kitty, you look like a right sweet girl," Cappy said. "Don't you think we ought to take you to the airport while you're still innocent and pure?"

"I'm not exactly innocent and pure. But if I were, what makes you think that would change, anyway?"

Cappy looked into Kitty's face. "Because you're a human being. Because Eve listened to that damn snake instead of stomping his head flat. Because we'll all sell our asses for the right number of greenbacks." He turned back to the road. "I hate helping spread the disease."

"You hush," Glory scolded. "Kitty, she the cook and the bus driver. That's all she gonna be. I'll attend to that."

"We'll see," Cappy replied. "Don't nobody want to be the cook when they can be the queen. That ain't human nature, sweetheart.

That boy driving, he could have stayed home and gone to school and played with his pecker. Now he's snatching up rattlesnakes like a fool."

Jubal frowned into the rearview mirror at Cappy. "School ain't everything. You never went."

"No, I didn't. I didn't have the fucking chance. But you did. You were in. And you just walked away."

"Things changed, Cap."

"No, you changed. Right now, you remind me of a greyhound. I never ran from nothing. I'd have gotten Darlene out here, somehow."

Jubal opened his mouth to argue, his face flushed and angry.

"Hush that," Glory hissed. "Miss Darlene will hear you. We're in this together. Kitty, maybe you ought to get out now."

Kitty felt a blush of excitement across her face, then a shiver at the base of her neck and down her spine. She was with people who cursed and argued and said what was on their minds. They talked of danger and disease, and of the threat of selling one's dignity for money. She found such harsh talk invigorating, not at all like the drone of her psychiatrist's babble. She knew then she wouldn't leave that bus unless she was dragged away. Kitty looked at Glory and shook her head. "No."

TOWARD MIDNIGHT, Jubal wheeled the bus into the parking lot of a convenience store. Cappy talked for a few minutes into a pay phone, nodding and scribbling on a piece of paper. He climbed back into the bus, opened the cooler, and took out a beer. "Had to talk to goddamn security first. Then the butler or whatever he was got on.

Talked like a British fairy. Finally Jasper's pervert buddy got on the line. I told him who we were. I swear he was slobbering into the phone.

"What did he say?" Jubal asked.

"He said, Come on down! Said we could even stay in the guest quarters tonight. Don't have to camp."

"Guest quarters?" Glory said. "I can already smell the hundred-dollar bills."

"Go another two miles," Cappy instructed Jubal. He tried to decipher his own scribbles. "You cross a bridge over a creek, then make a right. Then turn left into a driveway. He said it's the only one."

Jubal swung back onto the road. Cappy turned his beer up. He noticed Kitty watching him. "You drink beer, little miss?"

"Occasionally. I'm not quite legal age to buy it."

Cappy reached again into the cooler. "I'll buy it. You better start fortifying yourself right now." He handed her a can.

A few minutes later, Jubal braked the bus and turned onto a paved driveway that led up a hill. He braked once more when he reached a set of wrought-iron gates. A man in uniform came out of the gatehouse nearby. Cappy stood in the bus doorway.

"May I help you, gentlemen?" the security guard asked.

"I called. I ain't much of a gentleman."

"What is the nature of your visit, sir?"

Cappy indicated his companions on the bus. "We're The Last Great Snake Show."

The security man nodded. "You are expected." He went back into the gatehouse, and a moment later the two big gates swung open.

The bus entered and wound its way on a fissured road to the circular driveway of a sprawling three-story mansion. Even in the darkness, it was obvious that the place was past its prime: the paint on the porch columns was chipped, the mortar between the bricks deteriorating and dirty. The group exited the bus and approached the double front doors. Cappy, helping to support Darlene, rang the bell three times. A butler opened the door and with a minimum of words escorted them inside.

The house reminded Kitty of many a house in Wilmington, even her own. High ceilings, big windows, hardwood floors, mahogany banister. But the air here was stale, the paint faded, the wood worn and the polishes yellowed. The place was poorly lighted.

The butler led them upstairs to a wing with several bedrooms. He informed them that the master of the house was already asleep but that he would bring to each room a modest supper and drink. He arrived at Cappy and Darlene's room half an hour later with a tray of bread, cold ham, and cheese, a fifth of bourbon, and tumblers with ice.

Cappy stared at the label on the bottle, then uncapped it. "Beats the woods," he said, pouring whiskey into the tumblers.

HE WAS HAVING his dream again, and as always the images were as real as life. Smoke in his nose, heat on his face, men shouting, the plane bucking and hammering on her way down.

"We're going in!" the co-pilot yelled from the cockpit. "Get in crash positions."

Cappy sat up in bed. His face was sweaty. A weak light filtered through gauzy curtains. He panicked for several moments, trying to recall where he was. Then the memories filled him: the tornado, Darlene's injury, this ridiculous, hell-bent journey she had talked him into.

The window near the bed was open, and the breeze that spilled in was sweet and fresh. Birds were singing, a chorus of high and middle notes; Darlene's slow breath whistled softly through her lips as she slept beside Cappy. He needed to rise and empty his bladder, but he was reluctant to move. Darlene had mumbled in her sleep for much of the night, but now she seemed at peace, and Cappy did not want to wake her. His mind was still fuzzy from sleep and those dreams. He could feel last night's whiskey in his temples.

As dawn gathered in the room, Cappy could make out the ceiling, and the small chandelier above the bed. He imagined how grand the house must have looked years before, the paint fresh and the varnishes clear; how the chandelier must have caught the first light and fractured it into colors.

He eased himself out of the rough sheets and tiptoed into the small adjoining bathroom. The floorboards groaned beneath him. He urinated into the sink to avoid making noise, then rinsed the basin with water from an old, tarnished faucet.

When he returned to the bedroom, he heard a knock at the door. "Come in," he growled.

The door squealed as it opened slowly. The butler stood in the hallway. "The madam has asked that you join her downstairs for breakfast in fifteen minutes."

Cappy glanced at his watch.

"I realize that your people usually sleep till noon," the butler went on, "but we operate on real time in this household." He closed the door as slowly as he had opened it. Cappy could hear him knocking at another door. Darlene rolled onto her side.

"Fuck it." Cappy lowered himself to the floor beside the bed and pumped out his usual morning set of fifty push-ups. The floor creaked with each thrust.

Routine was the only thing that kept him sane these days. The world seemed to be going to hell faster and faster since he had retired from the Army. He had enlisted at eighteen, leaving behind his elderly parents, a dusty tenant farm, and twin headstones where a brother and sister had rested since a polio epidemic. He endured boot camp and jump school at Fort Bragg, then was shipped to Korea, where he won a Purple Heart. At the end of his first enlistment, he knew he had found a family, and he reenlisted. In the early years of the Vietnam War, he received a field commission to second lieutenant; he returned to Vietnam twice. When he retired in 1982, he had served for thirty years. On his dress uniform were three Purple Hearts, two Bronze Stars, and the Silver Star. But on his shoulders he carried only captain's bars. Throughout his career Cappy had had encounters with superior officers educated at VMI or West Point who knew war only through books. When he decked a full-bird colonel near the end of his last Vietnam tour, Cappy knew he'd never make major. "Captain" had more flair, anyway. He liked his nickname.

Cappy stood from his push-ups and flexed his arms. Darlene's eyes were open. He sat on the bed and touched her arm. "You sleep okay?"

"This place is strange," she said. "Feels like it's haunted by memories."

"Lurch just called us to breakfast."

Darlene looked into Cappy's eyes. "You had that dream again last night. I heard you talking. Why won't you tell me about it?"

"It's just a nightmare. Nobody ever remembers nightmares. Let me help you get dressed. I need some coffee bad."

THE BUTLER seated everyone except Glory at a large table with a lace tablecloth, china, and silverware. He directed Glory to a small table with a plastic plate and tin dinnerware in a corner of the room. The butler rang a little bell, and moments later a wizened old woman in formal dress entered the room and took the chair at the head of the table. Her dress, though clean and pressed, was faded and slightly tattered, as if it had been owned for many years. The woman looked to be at least ninety. Her eyes had the milky-blue cast of cataracts. When she smiled, her face split with hundreds of wrinkles.

"I'm so happy to have y'all here," she said. "Isn't that the way you say it down there? I like the way you people speak."

Cappy raised an eyebrow at Darlene.

The old woman leaned forward. "I know you don't like dining with nigras," she whispered, "but this is the best I could do. I'm just so happy to have visitors."

Glory looked up from her table. "What the hell!" she muttered. Darlene lifted her hand to quiet her.

"It's a pleasure to be your guest," Kitty told the woman. "You have a lovely house."

"It's historical, you know. Built before the Civil War—or what is it you people call it? The 'inconvenience,' I believe. Oh, I just loved *Gone With the Wind*. 'I don't know nothing about birthing babies, Miss Scarlett.'" The woman leaned forward again and pointed toward Glory. "Does she? Could she birth a baby? I'm sorry to have to seat you in the same room with a nigra."

"Maybe I'll just seat myself upstairs," Glory said.

"Oh, she's uppity. Isn't that the word you use, 'uppity'?"

Glory pushed back from her table. Darlene motioned for her to stay where she was. "Oh, she's uppity, all right," Darlene told the old woman. "She's uppity and doesn't know a thing about birthing babies. But she's part of the family. I share the breakfast table with her every morning."

"But I thought—I mean, you read so much about the South. I hope I haven't offended anyone." The woman lifted the bell from the table and jingled it. Within seconds, the butler appeared.

"Yes, madam?"

"Please set a place at our table for the nigra woman. She will be having breakfast with us."

"A GODDAMN LUNATIC," Cappy shouted. "That old woman is crazy as a loon." He was opening a can of Spam in his bedroom as the others watched. "Melba toast with cream cheese and smoked mussels. Plain yogurt with wheat germ. Hot tea! That ain't breakfast food. We used to do better than that in the field during combat."

Cappy emptied the Spam onto a paper plate. He sliced it with his pocketknife and put pieces of the meat on saltines. "Y'all eat up. Hell of a breakfast, ain't it. Spam and warm beer." He guzzled from his can. "Better than yogurt, though."

"She's probably getting senile," Kitty said. "She was just trying to be nice."

"Since when did you get to be a psychologist?"

Kitty blushed.

"Don't be so damn hateful," Glory told Cappy. "You ain't the only one who ate that stuff."

"I ain't going without lunch. You can bet on that. We're packing up and getting out of this place before the walls cave in. Cut our losses and go the hell home."

"Quit bellyaching, Cap," Darlene said from the bed. "She told us her son was on the way up."

"Do you think she really has a son? If she does, he ain't much at maintenance."

"She *has* a son."

The voice came from the door, as it was pushed open. In the doorway stood a tall, thin man in a dark suit. His hair was sparse and silver, his eyes a watery blue. The door opened wider and he stepped into the room. His eyes moved slowly from person to person; his top lip twitched. "You don't look very impressive to me," he said finally.

"And who might you be?" Cappy asked.

"Reginald Pearson."

"Are you the birthday boy?"

"I have a birthday in a few days, yes. I'm having a party."

"Well, we be the life of the party," Glory said. "We'll light your candle at both ends."

Reginald's eyes traveled the length of Glory's body. "Yes. I've been told that. Jasper said you put on quite a show."

"How do you know Jasper?" Jubal asked.

"We've had some business dealings."

"You connected with the movies too?"

"I was once. In more favorable years. I have to tell you that I don't really care for southerners."

Cappy tilted his head. "You don't have to love us. Just pay us."

Reginald looked from Cappy to the wall, at a spot where the paint was peeling. He chipped at the paint with a finger, making particles fall like dandruff. "I understand you can make fantasies come true?"

"Honey, if you can dream it up, we can make it come true," Glory said.

Reginald studied the bare spot on the wall. "I don't really like the South. No unions. All the labor has gone there. Without labor up here, the industries collapse. When I was a boy, this house was a monument to beauty. Now look at it. You know my mother is crazy, don't you?"

"I sort of got that hint," Cappy said.

"She wasn't always that way. These walls used to get a fresh coat of paint every two years. Now look at them. Your people did it."

"Look, man," Cappy said. "I'm just here to do a show, take our pay, and leave."

"You'll get paid. I'll have instructions for the party delivered at noon." The door squealed sadly as Reginald closed it behind him.

"AUNT BEA, my black ass," Glory said, holding aloft a flower-print dress three sizes too large that had just been delivered in a box with other clothes by the butler. "I can't be Aunt Bea."

"You're more Aunt Bea than you're Sheriff Taylor," Jubal said. "Somebody has to be her."

"Aunt Bea wouldn't wear no garter belt. It's a sin to even think such a thing."

"Look, it's just a show," Cappy said. "We'll be out of here in a few hours, heading west. I don't like it either. But we need the money."

"And Aunt Bea wouldn't act such a way," Glory said. "There has to be a few things sacred in the world."

Everyone had left Darlene resting and gone to Glory's room to look at the clothes and the script for the show. Besides Aunt Bea's dress, there were a sheriff's uniform, one for a deputy, and a yellow sundress.

"I reckon this be for Miss Helen Crump," Glory said. "I think I make a better Miss Helen."

"I think Kitty is the natural Miss Helen," Jubal said. "She don't have enough ass for Aunt Bea."

Glory scowled at Jubal, then turned to Kitty. "I don't know if you can act or not, but we need somebody to fill this dress. What you say I teach you the ropes."

Kitty's face was scarlet. "I—I can't dance. Maybe the waltz, that's all."

"The waltz! That must be some fancy orphanage you from."

"I've seen people waltz. Mostly in movies."

"I guess you be Miss Crump, then. Don't worry. I'll do the ass-shaking. White people can't dance, anyhow." Glory stared at the flowered dress. "I'm sorry, Aunt Bea, but it only a show. We got to take Miss Darlene home. You'd understand that."

AT SEVEN in the evening, cars began to climb the hill toward the mansion and park under the large elms in front. Each car carried a man not so different from Reginald—aging, reserved in behavior, dressed in a suit. A banquet room, which smelled of mothballs, of meat recently past its prime, had been set up with tables and linen cloths. Classical music, all selections from German composers, played softly from two stereo speakers. A buffet was spread with corned beef, cheese biscuits, raw vegetables and dips. The butler served as bartender, carefully measuring out shots of scotch. The guests steadily got drunk and drunker in this house whose best times were now left to memory.

DARLENE LAY on her bed in the bus. She had left the house against Cappy's protests, preferring her space on the bus to the musty-smelling guest bed. Glory, in her Aunt Bea costume, had come to check on her before the show. She lifted Darlene's chamber pot from the floor and went to empty it on the grass outside. Darlene heard cursing; Glory must have stumbled, maybe dropped the pot. Moments later, she was back on the bus.

"I'm sorry for all this," Darlene said. "I know you're not my maid or my nurse. You don't have to empty the pot. I'm not a cripple. I can empty it myself, or go in the house."

"Oh, hush now. I don't mind one bit. All the things you done for me these years." Glory set the pot down. "I couldn't ask Kitty to do it. She might throw up. Can't dance. Looks timid as a mouse." She fluffed the pillow under Darlene's head. "You sure you don't want to stay in the house? Got that big bed to lie in."

"I'm fine right here. That house smells like something that ain't been opened up for years."

"You right about that. I never smelled nothing so bad."

"You'll be out of there before you think, and I'll be right here, already looking west."

Glory sat down and took Darlene's hand in hers. "It's gonna be so pretty out there, Miss Darlene. I can close my eyes and see your lan'. We're gonna all be happy there."

Darlene squeezed Glory's hand. "I want you to promise me something. When this is all over, I want you to move on to something, beauty school, whatever you want to do. I don't want you ending up like me."

SHE HAD LEFT Oregon at sixteen, wrapped in the arms of a sailor, bound for a new life in the East. When the affair ended a year later, Darlene found herself penniless and alone in Jacksonville, North Carolina, a scrappy military town. She waited tables in restaurants, then was lured into the beer joints, where the tips were better. When topless dancing began in the early sixties, she gave up the tables and went big-time. Between the Marine bars in Jacksonville and the paratrooper haunts in Fayetteville, she made a living with her lithe, firm body that matched the income of many a college graduate.

Darlene met Cappy in 1963, when he slapped her on the rump after she came offstage; she backhanded him and bloodied his lip, then ended up sitting down and having a beer with him. They spent the next three nights together, before he shipped off for his first tour in Vietnam. Cappy replied to her letters only a few times, but Darlene nevertheless kept writing weekly, telling him what was happening in her life, advising him to keep his feet dry and his head low.

About every six months when Cappy was overseas, she would receive a package from him—a set of teakwood bowls from Thailand, a pewter stein from Switzerland, a German clock—something that had caught his eye while he was on leave. Always a week or so after Cappy got back in-country, he'd show up at the bar where she was working, and if there was a man in Darlene's life at the time, there wasn't anymore.

For twenty years, she strutted her stuff. She had a mind as pert as her breasts, and she saved her tips through all those years, never letting the men who came and went know of her banking practices. As she entered her forties and gravity began to affect her tips, she had enough of a nest egg to buy into a bar farther south, in Wilmington, on Front Street, where fistfights between patrons weren't as frequent as in the military towns.

Ten years later, the Wilmington downtown revitalization plan had no use for topless bars, and the future looked bleak for Darlene when the city forced her out. With a mind to change gears and open a restaurant, she gambled the last of her savings and bought a sprawling, two-story frame house overlooking the Cape Fear River. At first the crowds were good; people liked the home-style seafood and the pleasant view of the river. But when business declined, Darlene's old survival instincts surfaced. She began keeping the front door open past midnight, and served more beers than deviled crabs. Then she got a license for hard liquor and a jukebox. Word got out that Miss Darlene's was lax on the law, and that if she knew you, corn liquor could be bought there, as well as beer on Sunday mornings. Darlene rescued Glory from a street corner and moved her into a bedroom. She discovered Jubal doing his snake-catching act for tips on the boardwalk at Carolina Beach; he was working his way through school. Then she persuaded Cappy to buy in. They painted the place canary yellow and dubbed it The House of Joy. For two years it romped nightly except Sunday, reservations required, but not coat and tie.

The House of Joy might have stayed like any other honky-tonk, had not the movie business started to thrive in Wilmington. Film crews from the West Coast traveled there to shoot at a fraction of the usual cost. Nick Nolte and his cast came to The House of Joy one night, and word spread that Miss Darlene could show you a side of the South that didn't include mint juleps.

DARLENE TURNED her face from Glory to the light fading in the window. "I dreamed about my land last night."

"I bet that was a good dream."

"I dreamed I was standing on the shoreline looking out to sea, at the most glorious sunrise I ever witnessed."

"That's nice."

"But that's so strange."

"What's strange about a pretty sunrise?"

"I was standing on my land, Glory, looking out to sea. The sun doesn't rise in the west."

Glory's brow furrowed. Then she smiled. "You were just confused. Thinking you were back at The House of Joy. That place long gone, tore down by the hand of God. We traveling to a new land." She squeezed Darlene's hand and stood. "I gotta get ready. Never thought I'd be doing Aunt Bea."

She fluffed Darlene's pillows and spread a blanket over her legs before leaving the bus. Darlene watched her go, then closed her eyes.

As if snatching a fly from the air, Jubal practiced the motion, flashing his arm out again and again. It had been nearly a month since he had snagged a rattlesnake. He kicked the side of the bucket to make the rattler buzz; he was focused on that sound and an image of the snake, coiled and tense and ready. Flick! It was all there. Just reach out and seize it. But was he really laying siege or retreating, Jubal wondered. His words swirled through his head, repeating. . . .

People have asked me since I was little, "Boy, why do you like to play with them snakes?" I never had an answer that really suited even me. But on this trip I've done a lot of thinking. If I'm honest with myself, I'd say that I pick up rattlers more out of fear than out of anything brave.

Everyone I knew growing up worked at least a five-day week, and some more than that. They got their pay on Friday, and by Monday morning the bills had been tended to, a little money had been spent on some hunting gear or maybe a new dress. Families might go to the fish house and have a combination plate; single men would drink their fish plate. It was that way week after week, month after month, year after year.

I never knew my father. He died on a road one Saturday night. I grew up seeing my uncle's hands, callused and scarred and chapped from the salt air. If either man did any reading, I don't know about it. The world for them extended thirty miles out to sea, and another thirty inland. Once every summer, our families would caravan up to

Cherokee in the mountains and spend a night at the Blue Ridge Motel.

I was born with something different, and I'm not sure whether to call it a gift or cowardice. I wanted to know things in books and see places like the pictures in *National Geographic*. Not only did I not want to go out in a boat every morning and pull nets, I was scared that I couldn't. That I wasn't man enough to work like that, day in, day out, in a job that was drying up with the marshlands, for a paycheck and blistered hands. That one day I would just walk away, and be a failure in everyone's eyes.

The first time I picked up a canebrake rattler, I felt a power like electricity. People didn't pick up rattlesnakes; they chopped them to pieces with a hoe. If you picked up rattlesnakes and cottonmouths, you were different—maybe even a little crazy, or a lot, depending on who was watching. And if you were different—if you read books about herpetology, if you actually thought of going to college and maybe one day traveling to one of those places—expectations for you were different. Hell, anybody who played with snakes could be expected to want something different.

It sounds impossible that you could love and hate something at the same time. I love the land I was born on, but I've seen it suck so many people down like quicksand, till all they had were a few acres of marshland and more wishes than memories. My brother, he loved it, that coastland and the sun on the water. He loved it so much he came back, even when he had a way out.

I'm far from home and thoughts of college now, and I don't think this road will lead me back. If I had stuck with pulling nets, my arms would be stronger, and they wouldn't have let me down when I needed them most.

JUBAL KNELT on one knee in his snake-catching stance behind the curtain, in a uniform that was too big. It was a discard from the local sheriff's department, faded and torn, but clearly that of law enforcement, with a badge on the chest.

Cappy wasn't as lucky. His uniform was too small, tight around his waist, the trouser legs revealing his bare ankles. Glory wore her tent-sized dress open to show some cleavage; the fishnets and high heels hardly suggested Aunt Bea. She held a wicker shopping basket adorned with plastic flowers.

"Aunt Bea would roll over in her grave," she said. "Kitty, you look sweet, all tanned in that dress. Ain't nothing but eyes gonna touch you."

The four stood behind a curtain made from a roll of canvas, on which Jubal had hastily painted a scene resembling the Blue Ridge Mountains. On the other side of the curtain, the men in the audience were getting louder; the scotch must have been kicking in. A glass shattered on the floor.

Cappy inserted a cassette into a tape player. "At least the fool had his own music. This ain't exactly the stuff we played at The House of Joy."

Kitty nervously fingered the strap of her dress. "I get scared in front of people."

"Just scream when you see the snake," Jubal said. "Clutch your dress in the front and hike it up a bit."

Kitty blushed. "I'm the bus driver, remember."

"All right," Cappy said. "Let's do this and get out of this dump." He pointed to Jubal. "Don't do no fancy stuff and get your ass bit! Soon as we're done, I'll get the money and we'll split. This place gives me the creeps."

Cappy bent and tugged at his trouser legs, then reached and pushed the start button on the cassette player. The whistling theme to *The Andy Griffith Show* began. As it wound down, Glory took a mighty breath and stepped between the part in the curtain into the naked light of the ballroom. The men were silent, watching her as she walked to a plain wooden table at the edge of the stage. She set down her bag and spoke in a high-pitched voice.

"Oh, I better start making the biscuits now. Andy and Opie will be home soon, hungry as bears." She reached into imaginary shelves and drawers, put imaginary utensils on the table, then mixed the imaginary ingredients in a bowl. She bent over the table and kneaded dough, the top of her dress opening wider to reveal more of her breasts. Reginald and several other men leaned forward, but the room remained silent.

"Boy, it sure is hot in here," Glory said. "Making biscuits is the hottest work." She unfastened two more buttons, and the fabric slipped off her left breast. "It's just *so* hot in here. I think I'll have a little nip of sweet sherry. Andy don't know. Just a little nip."

Glory reached into her shopping bag and took out a sherry bottle filled with Kool-Aid. She turned the bottle up and gulped from it, then wiped her mouth with the back of her hand. "Now, that hit the spot. That hit the spot. Make me want to dance. Oh, it so hot in here."

She grabbed her dress and lifted the hem to the height of her garters, and swayed slowly. "What I need is some music. Let this dough rise."

Glory walked away from the table, and slipped one hand up the back of her thigh and pulled her dress up to her buttocks. With her other hand she turned the dials on an imaginary radio. "Yeah, some music I need. All this heat in here make me want to dance."

She returned to the table, swishing her dress as she moved her hips. She blew a kiss toward Reginald. "Yeah, this heat make me want to dance. Like I *said,* all I need is a little *music!*"

Quick steps were heard behind the curtain, Cappy scrambling for the cassette player. The next selection was "Ninety-nine Bottles of Beer on the Wall." Glory moved her hips in a circle.

Reginald stood and sang the words. By the time he reached bottle ninety-three, all the guests were standing and singing. At eighty-five bottles the singing had trailed off. Glory saw Cappy peering through the gap in the canvas. "Cut the music," she mouthed. She winked at Reginald, then fanned her face with her hand.

"Oh, my goodness. That sherry went straight to my head. I must have blacked out." She straightened and buttoned her dress. "Oh, goodness, that sherry is wicked, but the biscuit dough, oh, it just right. I'm gonna make Andy and Opie some pretty buttermilk biscuits."

Glory hummed and went back to kneading the imaginary biscuit dough. After a few moments, she peered toward the curtain. In a louder voice she called, "Yeah, like I said, the biscuit dough is just right." Another few moments passed. "Yeah. The damn biscuit dough is ready!"

A shrill scream came from behind the curtain. Cappy and Kitty ran through the part in the curtain, holding hands. Kitty screamed again.

"My goodness. What is wrong?" Glory shouted. "Y'all gonna make the dough fall."

"Aunt Bea, there's a great big rattlesnake out there in the front yard," Cappy said in his best Barney Fife voice. "What are we gonna do? It nearly bit Miss Helen."

Kitty stood rigid beside Cappy, staring at the floor. He tapped her sharply on the hip. Her eyes widened and she looked at him, then pulled her dress above her knees. Her face flooded crimson.

"Why don't you shoot it, Barney?" Glory said.

"Now Aunt Bea, you know I have only one bullet. What if I use it and some criminals come into town?"

Glory nodded vigorously. She shifted her eyes to Kitty, who was staring at the floor again. When Cappy tapped her hip again, Kitty gasped and blurted, "Call Andy. He'll know what to do."

Glory hurried to the side of the stage. She lifted an imaginary phone. "Clara, get me Andy, please. This is an emergency." She shifted the phone to her other ear. "Andy. There's a snake in the yard. It nearly bit Helen. You need to *get* over here." She hung up the phone. "Oh, everything will be all right now. Andy is on his way."

"Me and Helen will run out and guard the snake until Andy gets here," Cappy said.

"Well, don't look it in the eye. You know they say a snake can hypnotize you."

Cappy took Kitty's hand and led her offstage. Glory looked into the audience. "Andy will know what to do. Oh, a snake is an evil creature. If it wasn't for snakes, there wouldn't be any evil today. There certainly wouldn't be any sex."

Cappy pushed the start button on the tape player. Tom Jones's voice, and a song about a woman who takes in a sickly snake and nurses it to health, only to be bitten by it and told, "You knew I was a snake before you took me in."

Glory did a slow grind to the music. A four-foot-long rubber snake sailed over the top of the curtain, hit the stage, and skittered across the floor. Glory swooped down on the snake, lifted it, and instantly was on top of the table, where, for a few minutes, she undulated like a serpent. As the music ended, she tossed the rubber snake to Reginald, who caught it in both hands; the rubber skin was shiny with Glory's perspiration. Reginald stared at the toy for several seconds, then dropped it to the floor.

Glory hopped down from the table, slapping her face and shaking her head as if trying to awaken from a trance. "Oh, just the thought of a snake makes me dizzy. I must have had another one of my spells. Oh, my goodness."

Voices sounded from behind the curtain.

"Andy, over here."

"Hurry, Andy, that snake nearly bit me."

"I would have shot it, Andy. But you know I can't waste my only bullet."

Slowly, the curtain began to rise behind Glory. She pushed the table stage right. Jubal was crouched in his catching position with his side to the audience, the rattler coiled and buzzing before him. He inched his right hand toward the rattler's head, while waving his left to distract the snake. Three times the rattler struck, Jubal jerking backward each time to avoid the fangs, the snake recoiling instantly. On the fourth try, he got his catching hand within range, and then he struck.

He stood, lifting the snake by the head, his free hand locked around the midsection. Glory slumped to the floor in a mimed faint. Jubal walked toward the audience with the rattler above his head. He squeezed the snake's poison glands, and the animal gaped and squirted twin streams of venom in Reginald's direction.

Among the men in the audience, mouths were open, eyes reflected fear, envy, and dread. Reginald began the applause, measured and controlled, and louder than it had been for Glory.

"You got it, Andy!" Cappy ran onto the stage, carrying a bucket and a lid. Jubal dropped the serpent inside, and Cappy carried it away.

Kitty ran next onto the stage. "Oh, Andy," she cried. "You saved me."

They hugged, walked to where Glory lay, took her hands and helped her to her feet. Music started again, a recording of Marilyn Monroe singing "Happy Birthday" to President Kennedy. Glory straightened her wig and climbed on the table. She offered another dance, delivering pelvic thrusts to accent Marilyn's breathless words. The song over, she leaped from the table to the floor and went to Reginald's table. She mounted his lap, placed her hands on his shoulders, and rubbed her breasts against his face, now singing herself.

"Happy birthday, Reginald. If you weren't so cute, I'd spank you sixty times." She kissed his forehead and sprang back onstage, waving to the audience. "Good night, y'all. We love you!" She pivoted, still waving. "Bye-bye. Aunt Bea gotta go before she get another fainting spell."

Behind the curtain, Cappy was unplugging the cassette player. Jubal had stripped to the waist. Glory was about to duck behind the canvas when Reginald stood and shouted.

"I want the girl!"

Glory looked at him. "Say what?"

"I want some time in the bedroom. Jasper said that was part of the deal."

Several of the men in the audience were clapping. Reginald hauled himself onstage and faced Glory. "I want thirty minutes."

Cappy came from behind the curtain. "What's going on?"

"Reginald getting frisky," Glory told him.

"Show's over, buddy," Cappy said. "Give me my cash, and we'll be out of here."

"Some time with the girl," Reginald said. "I'm paying for it. Jasper said she would."

"That wasn't part of the deal," Cappy said.

"I've got the money. I make the deals. I want the girl for thirty minutes. Otherwise, you don't get a cent."

Glory exhaled heavily. "Look, Cap, this couldn't take more than a couple of minutes. Y'all go on and load up, and I'll be there in a little bit."

She took Reginald by the arm. "Come on, hot rod. I hope you got a strong heart."

He stared at Glory, then pulled his arm out of her grasp. "Not you!" He spat out the words. "I want the girl."

Realization slapped Glory like a cold hand. Rage swelled in her chest. "Look here, pop, you want your wick wet, that's my department. Not some skinny-ass little white girl. She wouldn't know what to do, anyway." She reached for Reginald's arm. "Let's get it on. Time's wasting."

He stepped backward, a sneer on his face. "Frankly, the idea of you and me together makes me nauseous."

"What kinda talk is that, buddy?" Cappy said. "You said you wanted thirty minutes. The clock is running."

"You said you fulfill fantasies," Reginald answered. "Well, my fantasy is to rebreed the South. Improve the gene pool. Miss Crump would be a good beginning. I don't want a sweaty black whore."

Glory's hand streaked out, and she hit Reginald hard across the cheek. He slumped to one knee. Reginald waved the butler and a guard forward. "They're attacking me!" he screamed. "Get them out of here. They're attacking me!"

The two men came over, and Reginald stood up.

"Get the gal and head for the bus," Cappy told Glory. "Jubal, get your young ass on out here."

Glory did as she was told. "Kitty," she said, "grab that boom box. We got to leave here."

"What's going on?"

"Ain't time to explain. Grab that boom box and follow me to the bus. Get the keys out and start it up."

Jubal came to Cappy's side. "What the hell happened?"

"Reginald's dick got hard for Miss Crump."

"You don't fuck Miss Crump!" Jubal said.

"Damn right you don't."

The butler and the guard were still near Reginald, their fists balled. Blood spotted his bottom lip. "Grab these men," he shouted. "They attacked me. I'm calling the police."

"Hey, look, fellows," Cappy said. "We're not wanting any problems. We'll just mosey on out of here."

"Detain them!" Reginald yelled. "I command you!"

The butler raised his arm and started for Jubal. He was only a step away when Jubal lifted his left arm. "Hey, wait a second," he said. "Did you know there was a trick in how I caught that rattler?" He moved his arm out to the side. "Let me show you."

The butler's eyes flicked to Jubal's decoy hand for only an instant, but that was all Jubal needed. He flashed a right hook into the man's jaw, then hit him with a flurry of hooks and jabs. The security guard went for Cappy but was met with a kick in the belly.

The punching and gouging that ensued lasted a minute or two. When Reginald flailed his arms wildly, Cappy downed him with a jab to the chin. Jubal dropped his opponent belly-down on the floor, then joined Cappy to bring the guard to his knees. Cappy gave the man one last punch that rocked him on his behind.

Jubal grabbed the rattlesnake bucket, and they bolted for the front door. The bus sat idling across the lawn with the headlights on. Glory, still dressed as Aunt Bea, stood beside it, holding open the door to the storage compartment. A high screech from the house swallowed the night sounds: Reginald had activated the security alarm.

Jubal slid the snake bucket into the storage area, slammed the door shut, and latched it. He followed Glory and Cappy onto the bus. Kitty was at the wheel, calf eyes staring from a white face.

"Go!" Jubal shouted. He pulled the lever and closed the door behind him.

The bus lurched to a start, rocking back and forth. The transmission groaned as Kitty shifted gears.

"Hell of a show, wasn't it?" Jubal said.

Kitty was in third when she approached the closed front gates. The security man ran out of the gatehouse, waving his arms.

"Hit it!" Cappy held the back of Kitty's seat.

"How can I? The gates are closed!"

"Don't slow down." Cappy extended his leg and pressed his foot on top of Kitty's, flooring the accelerator. The bus burst through the gates.

"You all right, Darlene?" Cappy shouted.

"I'm breathing," she answered from her bed.

Kitty braked and turned onto the highway. Her knuckles were white on the steering wheel. "What happened in there?"

"We had the grand finale," Jubal answered. "We're probably wanted in this state now."

"I wouldn't joke about it," Cappy said. "We might not get out of here. I was counting pretty hard on getting paid."

"I wouldn't spend that man's money," Glory said. "I'd eat dirt first."

"We might be doing that," Cappy replied.

The bus backfired twice as Kitty accelerated, the reports like warning shots fired into the pitch-black sky.

DAWN WAS A THIN RED LINE on the eastern horizon when Cappy walked out of the bus into the chill air. The breeze smelled strongly of diesel fuel and the smoke belching from the exhausts of the semis at the interstate rest stop. Cappy had directed Kitty to park there sometime after midnight. She had fallen asleep only minutes later. Cappy had gone to the rear of the bus to check on Darlene; he'd tucked her in, kissed her forehead. When he returned to the front, Jubal and Glory were in their dreams. He had lain awake most of the night, and even his brief sleep was fitful.

He walked to a picnic table in a grassy area and lit a cigarette, inhaled a few times, then blew smoke out long and slow. He pulled out his wallet and counted the bills: sixty-three dollars in all. The gas tank was nearly empty and would require about thirty dollars to fill; the bus was getting only about ten miles to the gallon. Denver was a two-day drive, and after the last fiasco, he wondered whether they should even go there.

The cigarette eased only a bit of the aching in Cappy's jaw and fists. One of his eyes was swollen and black, and a crusty cut split the middle of his chin. He had jammed the middle finger of his right hand on that last haymaker; his left had two teeth cuts. In the weak light, chilled and hurting, Cappy felt old and forlorn, the weight in his mind as heavy as that in his limbs.

I KNOW how Atlas must have felt with the whole damn world on his back. I'm feeling that way right now, on this rattletrap bus, with Darlene sicker than she lets on and no money to help her with. What bothers me most is that I've got my back to the South, and I don't feel the calling.

I left home to go fight people who I believed wanted to take from me what I and my friends had sweated for. Each time I went off to war, I carried a little plastic bag filled with dirt scooped from where I was living, a good-luck charm you could call it. I'd be under fire, and whether it was the goddamn Chinese or the VC, I'd swear those sons of bitches weren't taking my dirt. Not my yard, not my town or state, and certainly not my country. Maybe it was just luck, and if there's a God, maybe it was Him, but I always came back.

I can't be mad at Darlene for this weight I feel. All the shit from me she's put up with all these years, all the promises I haven't kept. She just wanted something good and clean to go to, something that didn't smell of stale beer and cigarette smoke. Carolina was getting pretty fucked, anyway. Too many damn people moving in. And now I'm leaving home again, but the enemy ain't overseas anymore. I ought to be digging my foxhole at the Mason-Dixon line.

I guess I don't have much right to bitch. I been selling my soul for the last few years to perverts and rich people simply for the greenbacks. I can't say I'm much better than the developers and realtors. But dammit, I did try for a long time. I fought for this country, I carried my sack of dirt and shot the enemy and got shot. But I wonder now if it was worth it. Folks don't seem to care about the land no more, the fields and farms and woods and marshes. They want a nice house on a half-acre and a car that ain't scratched and a VCR so they won't have to watch the news and see that most people don't have as much as them.

It's late to start caring now. I think I know what's up ahead, and that will end my concern about what's behind me.

GLORY HEARD ONLY SILENCE from Darlene's room. She lay on her mattress, still tired, but unable to ignore her bladder any longer, and wondered whether Darlene was awake, and whether she should see if Darlene needed anything.

Glory recalled her bedroom at The House of Joy, the red satin sheets so cool and comfortable compared with the bare mattress she lay on now.

She'd earned that luxurious bed. She'd sweated for it. She remembered how her journey had begun.

AFTER HIGH SCHOOL, there was no place to go but work. College was even further than the moon. Mama, she was sick with the blood sugar, and Daddy would come around once a year. I tried it straight for a while, but the hormones had been good to me, and I had a collection of curves that made men turn their heads. The only way I could go with a man I didn't know was to drink first, and in a couple of years, the drinking had pulled me way down. Way, way down. I was working a street corner one night when the wine got the best of me, and I ended up hugging a street pole with the dry heaves.

This car passed, then backed up, and I thought, Oh no, I ain't in no shape for this right now. A woman parked and got out and looked at me. Lord, she was pretty, jet-black hair and high cheekbones—that's the Indian blood in her—and the greenest eyes, eyes like jade.

"You okay?" she said to me.

And I said, "Do I look okay?"

I don't know what Miss Darlene saw in me, but she took me to a little restaurant and bought me a burger and some coffee, and the next week I started waiting tables at this little topless bar she owned, and drinking Pepsi-Cola instead of Thunderbird.

Oh, I was Miss Darlene's nigger at first. She was paying me minimum wage and working me hard. But she gave me a little room in the back where I could sleep. I started watching all them white gals up on that stage, and I knew I could do that. Do it better. One night I just stepped up there, and from then on, the men came to see me. Ain't it a hoot, live your whole life having to do double 'cause you black, 'cause you look a little different from the white people usually doing the paying. Then, all of a sudden, the white men flock in that bar 'cause I *was* black and different from what they used to. They know, like ol' Jasper would shout, the blacker the berry, the sweeter the juice.

There's many people would say what I do is sinful. My mama would. But the good Lord gave me certain gifts, and a gift is to be used. It was a whore that stood the longest beside Christ. Anyway, I don't plan to be this way much longer. . . .

THOUGH SHE FELT some guilt too, Glory could not deny the cold pit of anger she felt inside her heart. Days earlier, when she had boarded the bus in Wilmington, she was only six weeks away from a bona fide degree in cosmetology. For months she'd had her eye on that empty shop in the west quarter, where most of the black folks lived. She'd already talked to a man about a lease. She was going to open a beauty parlor where she could fix hair and do manicures. She'd have a full appointment book and a regular clientele, and between the shampoo basin and the dryer, they would discuss men and soap operas and how young people nowadays were out of control. Of course, on the few slow days she'd allow a couple of walk-ins, girls with eyes full of fire and dreams, and when the elderly women were nodding under the dryer, Glory would lean and whisper in a girl's ear and tell her about the days at The House of Joy, when she used to take it all off. The girl would look shocked at first, then grin, and say, "Miss Glory, you sure like to joke around. You're a successful businesswoman, probably ain't never even tasted a beer."

GLORY'S MOTHER laid the sack of flour and the canned goods on the wooden counter of the country store. The store smelled of ripe hoop cheese and Black Flag fly spray. Mr. Jim, the owner, an aging man with fuzzy white hair and a big gold front tooth, stood behind the counter, a pencil stuck behind his ear. Beside her mother, Glory stared into a glass case filled with gumdrops and jawbreakers and other penny candies.

"I like to charge it, please," Glory's mother said. She looked up quickly at the owner, then dropped her head. She was a slight woman, thin to the point of being bony. Her hair was bound up in a bandanna, and she wore an old dress.

"God damn, Lucinda. You been charging it for two weeks. I need some cash."

"The check be coming tomorrow."

"Then come back tomorrow, if you ain't got nothing to trade today. You got something to trade, we can do business."

Silence hung thick in the store. Glory's mother nodded. Mr. Jim smiled. He reached into the candy case and picked out a jawbreaker. "Here, gal," he told Glory. "Go out and play in the yard."

Glory hesitated. Her mother turned and motioned with her head. "I'll be with you in a minute." Glory went out and walked to the bench in the shade of a willow tree. She popped the candy into her mouth, rolled the sweetness on her tongue. Two yellow jackets buzzed around her, attracted by the scent of sugar. Glory swatted at them, then leaped to her feet and trotted toward the store. The smell of Black Flag was better than getting stung. At the screen door she paused. Through the film of wire, she saw Mr. Jim leaning against the wall behind the counter. His eyes were closed and his ample belly moved in and out. Glory could not see her mother.

"Yeah, that's it," Mr. Jim said. "Yeah. Yeah."

Glory stepped back from the door and looked toward the shade tree. She pushed the jawbreaker against the roof of her mouth. The sun was hot on her bare shoulders. She saw a car pass the store, a big shiny station wagon. Another family probably on the way to Myrtle Beach, the back of the car loaded with beach balls and towels and swimsuits, and a picnic basket packed with fried chicken and potato salad and sodas.

She watched the car zip by, then fade to a spot on the horizon. Many summer afternoons when there were no butter beans to shell or weeds to chop in the garden, she had stood beside that same road and watched the cars speed by, filled with people who had their eyes straight ahead, seeing miles beyond the sweet gums and pines to white sand and saltwater. Glory would begin twirling whenever a car drew near, and move her head from side to side, thinking, "Look at me. Look at me. I am Glory, and I have a pretty name. Look at me. I am alive."

Occasionally a driver would toot the horn; once a paper cup sailed out a car window and exploded at her feet, drenching her dusty legs with cold, sticky soda. "Look at me. I have a name. I have a face and hands and toes."

The red panties arrived one morning in a sack of used clothes the social worker had brought. Bright red, with lace around the leg and waist bands. Glory held them, sleek and cool as snakeskin, against her cheek. Beat the heck out of the usual ones she wore. That afternoon by the roadside she lifted the front of her skirt as a car neared her; she saw a boy's face pressed against the window. His teeth were very white.

"Shit!"

Mr. Jim's voice pulled Glory's mind away from the fading station wagon.

"Give you some money? Shit. You ought to be paying me!"

Glory turned toward the dark doorway. She heard Mr. Jim laugh, but the sound was mean. "Pay you, like hell. I wouldn't pay your ugly-ass daughter."

She spit the jawbreaker into the sand.

SHE WASN'T SURE why she and Miss Darlene had gotten so tight over the years. Glory had nursed Darlene through a bad case of the adult mumps, which wasn't pretty. She'd worked hard. Maybe their bond was in the faith they both carried: Darlene, that one day she and the Captain would settle down and live out their old years quietly; Glory, that everyone was a child of the Lord, and that doing better was only a step away from the desire to do better. And now, here she was, lying on a bare mattress with nothing to make her rise to another day but a full bladder and a promise to a dying woman.

GLORY EMERGED from the bus, looked about, and spied Cappy. "Gotta pee like a racehorse," she said, passing him and continuing to the ladies' room at the rest stop. By the time she was back, Cappy had nearly finished another cigarette.

"Let me look at that chin," she said, pinching the cut between two fingers.

Cappy pulled back. "Damn it, Glory. You're hurting me."

"You acting like a baby. Hold still. You get infection in there, your head be swollen like a balloon."

Cappy held still while Glory looked closely at the cut. "He got you a good one."

"Sucker had a ring on his finger. He was the one on his butt when we left, though."

"I'll get the alcohol and a Band-Aid. You ought to put some ice on that eye."

"Glory, how much money you have squirreled away?"

"'Bout what a squirrel could tote. Twenty dollars."

"We've got a lot of miles between here and Denver. No guaranteed payday when we get there. We need gas and food, and Darlene needs her prescriptions filled."

Glory sighed. "The good Lord will provide, Cap. We're on a mission. I know that."

"She's getting weaker every day. We ought to turn that bus around and go home."

"Home to what? A pile of rubble."

"She's going to die out here."

"Maybe. But she's going to see her dream. That's better than laying up in a hospital bed. Miss Darlene needs to go out there. I can see it in her eyes."

"I hope her eyes know the road out there. Right now I'm feeling as lost as Moses."

"You picking the wrong hero, Cap. I look at you like David, and right now you bending down to pick up that stone."

THE SCRAMBLED EGGS were cooked until they were dry, the bacon was flaccid, but Kitty had managed to brew a decent pot of coffee. Everyone but Darlene sat at the picnic table eating in silence, considering the financial situation as Cappy described it to them.

"Just don't let on to Darlene," he advised. "She's got enough on her mind."

Jubal slurped from his plastic cup. "What if we were to set up a little sideshow in one of these small towns. I used to make sometimes a hundred dollars a day letting people see my snakes at the parking lot outside supermarkets."

"We'd have to have a permit to set up on public property," Cappy answered.

"We'll find us a supermarket and ask permission. Heck, we get Glory involved, we might make five hundred."

"We might get thrown in jail too."

Kitty had been chewing her food quietly. She knew she needed more than a few cooking lessons. She liked her coffee, though; it had just the right balance of sugar and milk and heat.

She still felt disgust at having lifted her skirt in front of those leering men at the mansion. She had never been around people who lived so crudely, who used so much profanity. Yet she'd sensed a delightful wildness when she first climbed into the bus. This was like an adventure novel, with something unexpected and dangerous in every chapter. By God, now she was even driving the bus!

She wondered how much gas the bus needed to get to Denver. She stood and excused herself, then started for the rest room.

Cappy helped Darlene from the bus to a lawn chair beside the picnic table. Glory handed her a cup of coffee. A hefty portion of eggs remained, and several strips of bacon, but after glancing toward the rest room, Glory dumped the food and relit the stove. She cracked a couple of eggs into a bowl.

"You don't have to cook special for me," Darlene complained. "Why'd you throw away those eggs?"

"Them eggs needed to be thrown away," Glory said. You don't need to choke to death 'fore you see your lan', she thought.

"The girl doesn't exactly strike me as being very worldly," Darlene said.

"Oh, Kitty is gonna learn. I ain't the cook. Everybody got to pull their weight around here. She been locked up in an orphanage all her life. Probably had to eat mush for breakfast."

"I don't think she ate much of anything," Cappy said. "Thin as she is."

The beaten eggs sizzled when Glory poured them into the pan. She let them sit for thirty seconds, then flipped them to the other side for another thirty seconds. Kitty was just emerging from the rest room when Glory handed Darlene a perfect browned omelet.

"You shouldn't hog all the eggs," Glory addressed Cappy as Kitty neared the table. "Miss Darlene gotta eat too."

"What the hell?" Cappy said.

Kitty greeted Darlene, then took a deep breath. "Hey, everyone. You won't believe what I found."

"Hope it was money," Cappy said.

"How'd you know? Two hundred-dollar bills." She held up the bills. "They were on the floor in the rest room."

Cappy shifted his eyes from the money to Darlene, then back. "You just found that?"

"Yes." Kitty fought to keep her voice steady. "On the floor beside the toilet. The gods have smiled on us."

"Thank the Lord!" Glory cried. "I told you, Cap. He was taking care of us."

"More like some trucker lady," Cappy answered. "Dropped her jeans and out it fell. I bet she's in a tizzy now."

"Reckon we ought to ask around?" Glory said. "It ain't ours, really."

"Let me see those," Darlene said. Kitty handed her the money. Darlene held the bills to her nose and sniffed. "These are new bills. Still smell like the bank. I don't think this money has been carried around in a trucker's pocket." Darlene stared past the money into Kitty's eyes. Kitty held the stare for only a second.

"Probably a tourist," Jubal said. "Somebody who's a hundred miles from here by now. I say we keep it and consider ourselves lucky."

"The good Lord sent it as a sign," Glory said. "Kitty, honey, this morning you His messenger."

"I think she is indeed." Darlene still stared at Kitty.

THE FLAT PRAIRIE of Kansas slipped by, the sky a great cathedral above the bus. When afternoon came, the western sun was a big orange ball through Kitty's shades. While Cappy snored on his mattress and Glory read the *National Enquirer*, Jubal sat beside Kitty and talked to her.

"What was it like growing up in an orphanage?"

"It wasn't so bad. It wasn't like *Oliver Twist* or anything."

"Who's Oliver Twist?"

"Oh, he's a character from a book. I was well taken care of. I went to school like any other kid. I want to go to college one day," Kitty said. "Did you go?"

"Naw. I thought about it for a while. I actually took some classes." Jubal shrugged. "It didn't work out."

"What did you study?"

Jubal looked out the window. "Marine biology. I was gonna try to save the coastline of North Carolina. I grew up on the water. When I was little, you could eat raw oysters right out of the creeks. Better not now. All that development. There's an island in the mouth of the Cape Fear River where I used to camp when I was a kid. Nothing there but birds and snakes and trees. If I was a millionaire, I'd buy it and then never cut a single tree."

"What was it called?"

"Boar Island. Ain't no wild boar on it, but I caught my first scarlet king snake there. Trouble is, the island *is* owned by a millionaire. Some asshole developer. Five years from now, there will be condos all over it. It'll be just like Bald Head. Retired Yankees living where there was once just forest and egrets."

"Not if I'm alive!" Kitty blurted. "I mean, if I could do anything to stop it, I would."

"You'd have to own it or be rich enough to buy it. That's about the only way you could save it. I doubt you're the unsuspecting heir to millions."

Kitty tightened her grip on the steering wheel. "You never know what's possible. You never know."

"I used to believe in that American Dream stuff. Even in miracles. I don't anymore."

"Tell me more about the island." Kitty's voice was low, wistful.

Jubal swallowed, then tilted his head back and closed his eyes. He opened them and stared through the windshield. He began slowly. His vivid memories of the Carolina marshlands were far stronger than his ability to put them into words.

$\star$ $\star$ $\star$

LIKE TWIN PORTALS into hell, the cottonmouth's eyes glowed red in the bright beam of the headlamp. The snake had frozen when the light found it, six inches of neck thrust above water, head as massive as a man's fist. A yard of body lay submerged in the tepid water of the Cape Fear River, where, until disturbed, the snake had been hunting minnows and frogs.

"He's a whopper," Jubal said. He was poised on his knees in the front of a wooden skiff. "Bring her in slow." Jubal kept his headlamp in the snake's eyes, blinding the animal to their approach.

In the rear of the boat, his uncle Tommy throttled the motor down until the boat barely glided forward. He swatted at the mosquitoes around his head. The low hum of the motor was barely audible over the night creatures singing their praise to a full moon that had turned the reeds along the shore to silver: bullfrogs carrying the bass, owls hooting back and forth from cypress tops, whippoorwills joining in the swamp symphony, and the tenor of mosquitoes and peeper frogs.

Jubal and his uncle had been on the river for three hours, since nightfall. From bush hooks baited with chunks of eel and suspended from willow branches above the water, they had taken nearly twenty pounds of catfish, now in the skiff. A burlap sack contained two dozen frogs they had gigged along the sandbar where Bear Creek flowed into the river. Inside a white feed sack were a dozen water snakes. Another sack, marked with red tape, contained three fat cottonmouths.

The skiff was within ten feet of the snake when Jubal put his left hand on the bow and leaned forward, his right arm extended beyond the keel. "Real slow, Tommy," Jubal said. "I want this bad boy."

With the expertise from hundreds of catches, the man inched the skiff forward. The light was fixed in the serpent's eyes. Jubal leaned farther from the bow, his hand poised, thumb and forefinger wide apart to the side of the beast. He heard a bobcat screech upriver but he remained rock-steady, drawing his hand toward the snake as the distance between them narrowed. When the angles were just right, Jubal closed his hand with a fluid and fleeting movement around the snake's neck and snatched it from the river. The serpent came up writhing and slinging water, its mouth gaping. Jubal lifted it into the boat, his free hand clasping the creature's thick midsection. Inches from his fingers, twin fangs squirted golden venom into the air.

"Hot damn," Jubal shouted. "Ain't it a hog!"

"Don't drop that son of a bitch," Tommy warned.

Jubal was holding nearly four feet of poisonous reptile. The snake tried to twist and bite, but the young man's arms were locked into place. Already Tommy was untying the sack with the red tape. He shook the bag a few times, then opened it. Jubal put the cotton-mouth in, tail first. When only the neck and head showed, he released the serpent as quickly as he had caught it, jerking his hand backward. Tommy twisted the sack closed and bound it with a length of rope.

"You're one crazy fool," Tommy said, after he had placed the sack on the deck and sat down. He fumbled for a cigarette. "I'd rather pick up a lit stick of dynamite."

Jubal laughed. "Everything's in the motion. Besides, all I see are dollar bills." From an ice chest, Jubal took a Mountain Dew and cracked it open, then turned the can up. "One more night, and we'll have enough snakes to take to the zoo. I told George we'd bring them a load by Thursday."

A match hissed as Tommy lit his cigarette. The flame illuminated the thin face of a man in his late forties, etched with the lines of a hard life. "Hand me a beer," he said.

Jubal fished through the ice. He tossed the can to Tommy and sat down facing him. He inhaled deeply the summer air, stewed with brackish water and mud and lush vegetation. Heat lightning flared against the horizon.

"You ought to leave these damn snakes alone and get back to your books. Since you were knee-high, all you ever talked about was how you were gonna be a scientist. You were gonna save Green Swamp."

"There's places beyond these swamps, Tommy, places I want to see."

Tommy grunted. "Shit, the first time I got out, I found myself being shot at in the middle of a rice paddy. I like it just fine here, thank you." He lifted his can and drank hard.

Jubal stared into the night sky. The thick air and moonglow allowed only the brighter stars to shine through. He focused on the brightest one. "You know, tomorrow it'll be a year since Andy died."

Tommy drew on his cigarette. "I miss him too, boy."

Jubal talked softly, his mind on the memory of his brother. "If he'd just stayed gone, he'd be living today. The Braves wanted him. He had to come back to this water. I made some promises."

"I ain't asking you to go back on your promises. I do know this, though. Damn cottonmouths and rattlers will kill you dead as drowning. You better quit that shit at The House of Joy. Leave that stage to the tits and ass. You don't, you're liable to be buried deeper than your brother."

"I know snakes. It's like you and a trawling net. If you know something well enough, it's not dangerous. That was Andy's problem. He should have stayed gone."

"He'd have come back sooner or later. This is home. Thinking of here is what kept me going when the shit got bad in 'Nam."

Jubal stared at the lights of a larger boat traveling upriver. "Maybe that's what I need. A good war to put things in perspective."

Tommy spit tobacco juice into the water. "What I see in your face lately, son, I think you're in a battle right now."

JUBAL WAS PULLING a shift at driving when the exit sign for Hays, Kansas, appeared.

"We might as well call it a day," Cappy told him. "I need to fill Darlene's prescriptions."

Jubal left the interstate, and turned south toward the town on a four-lane boulevard lined with the usual fast-food restaurants and strip malls. He pointed out a small campground they could return to for the night. When he pulled into the parking lot of a shopping center, Glory and Kitty woke from their naps; both of them squinted at the red sky and asked where they were.

"Hays, Kansas," Jubal announced. "As a sign back there said, home of the Prairie View Academy for Boys. I smell a snake show."

"I wish I smelled some supper," Glory said.

Jubal wheeled into a parking space, turned off the engine, then set the emergency brake. Cappy pulled out his wallet and handed a hundred-dollar bill to Kitty.

"You found it. Might as well be in charge of spending it. You three go get some groceries. I'll get Darlene's medicine. Bring back some change."

"GIRL, you got some high tastes for someone trying to stretch a dollar," Glory told Kitty after only a few minutes in the store. "I mean, I like nice things, but the Cap, he'll blow a fuse. He wanting quantity, not quality."

"I'm sorry," Kitty said. "I don't know anything about cooking oil."

Glory traded the olive oil Kitty had taken from the shelf for lard. "You'll learn. You didn't have a mama to watch shop like I did. This ol' pig fat ain't good for the heart, but the tongue like it. It cheap too."

Glory had already exchanged Kitty's butter for margarine, her chopped sirloin for hamburger. She had traded the ready-to-fry, frozen hash browns for a ten-pound bag of raw potatoes. The cart was nearly full when they reached the checkout counter. Glory had kept track of the total in her head. "We close to a hundred dollars, but not quite. Least we got food for a week."

"I never knew you could get so much food for under a hundred dollars," Kitty said. "Esther used to spend . . ."

"Who's Esther?"

"Oh . . . a woman who cooked at the orphanage. She bought the food."

"I bet she wasn't buying chopped sirloin. You got too much an eye for the fancy, Kitty."

"I never did much shopping."

Jubal arrived and dumped two packs of frankfurters into the cart.

"You found some chicken dogs," Glory said.

"I had to search. They're into beef out here."

"I never heard of chicken hot dogs," Kitty said. "Is that your favorite kind?"

"Not necessarily mine. These are mostly for the snakes."

"The snakes?"

"You'll see later."

The middle-aged man in front of them at the checkout counter turned and stared at Glory. When she smiled at him, he returned a frown. Glory began putting their purchases onto the belt. The man kept staring at them while waiting for his receipt. His eyes went from the food to Glory, then to Jubal and Kitty. "You people like to eat cheap, don't you?"

"Cheap is what you make it," Glory answered.

The cashier grinned and grasped the bucket of lard. "This is called soul food, Henry. Ain't you up with the times?"

The man snorted as he lifted his bag. He looked at Glory. "Around here, we call it nigger food."

Jubal stiffened, then tried to squeeze past Glory.

She gripped his arm tightly. "Let it go, baby," she said. "I grew up hearing that word. Reckon folks are the same 'round here."

WITH THE MOON well above the treeline, Darlene sat in a lawn chair with a blanket on her legs, while Cappy studied the road map. Over the camp stove, Glory coached Kitty in the art of making dinner. A can of green beans was open on the picnic table, and biscuits awaited cooking in a skillet.

"You see, Kitty," Glory said, "a tablespoon of this lard in those ol' beans makes them wonder beans. You be swearing your granny made them. You probably never knew your granny."

Kitty was trying to concentrate on the cooking, though she was distracted by Jubal. He sat on an upturned bucket holding a rattler by its head with his left hand, the snake's coils in his lap. After wetting a chicken frank with his saliva, he slowly poked it down the snake's throat until his fingers reached the fangs, then pushed the frank out of sight with a smooth stick. He slid the food down further, into the serpent's belly, with his thumb and forefinger. Already Jubal had fed a king snake, a rat snake, a coachwhip, and a banded water snake.

"Now I'm gonna put a little lard in this Hamburger Helper," Glory continued. "Make it Wonder Hamburger Helper."

Kitty's eyes moved from the shiny grease to Jubal, who was spitting on another frank. "Why does it have to be chicken franks?" Kitty asked him.

"You ever seen a snake eat a cow? Most of these snakes eat birds in the wild. You have to feed them something they're used to or they'll spit it up."

He took a four-foot snake from a pillowcase, where it had been separated from the other reptiles. Kitty stared at the serpent, its skin a mottled gray and wrinkled, not colorful and tight like the other serpents'.

"What's wrong with that one?" she asked. "It looks sick."

Jubal shook his head. "No, not sick. Watch."

Jubal scratched the snake's head with his fingernail. A sliver of gray skin curled back.

Kitty gasped. "You're hurting it!"

"No. I'm helping it. This is a corn snake. It's ready to shed its skin, but this traveling has dried it out."

Slowly Jubal stripped the dead skin from the snake's head. Circling the snake's body with his thumb and index, he peeled the skin down and inside out.

"My God!" Kitty gasped. "It's beautiful." The snake's true colors were revealed—vibrant reds, black, and shades of cream, gleaming in the lantern light. "I can't believe the change."

Jubal smiled. "Kinda like being reborn. Cap could use a good shedding."

Cappy grunted. "You could use some manners."

Kitty set the table with paper plates, a napkin folded beside each setting, and plastic utensils properly arranged, fork to the left, knife and spoon to the right. Cappy helped Darlene to the table, while Glory served.

Darlene studied her place setting. "That must have been a fine orphanage, Kitty, to teach a young woman such proper table etiquette."

"Jubal, you wash your hands 'fore you sit down here," Glory said. "Snake germs all over you."

Everyone was too hungry to talk much. Seconds were being passed around when Jubal started speaking. "I think we're in a good town to do a show. There's that prep school here, a lot of bored teenage boys. Well-to-do bored teenagers."

"We don't have a permit," Cappy reminded him.

"We're on private property. We'll talk to the campground owner, tell him we'll give him a cut. It's secluded back here. We could be set up and ready to go by tomorrow night. Be like an old-time county fair."

"Yeah, but in front of young boys," Cappy said. "We could get busted."

"Yum," Glory interjected. "Young boys!"

"I could tell fortunes," Darlene offered.

"Darlene, you ain't never told fortunes," Cappy said.

"I can now."

Cappy stared in thought at his plate. "We have a day to spare. The money sure wouldn't hurt." He looked at Jubal. "How do you suppose we get a group of those boys in here?"

Jubal grinned. "I saw a pool hall a half-mile up the road. There was a bunch of preppie-looking cars parked out front. Me and you could go play a game of eight-ball."

"Lead the way."

GLORY EASED HERSELF into a lawn chair. She watched Kitty washing the dishes in a plastic pail. She might know how to set a fancy picnic table, but it didn't look as if she had done much dishwashing, the way she dropped things and splashed suds.

Huh, Glory mused. Everybody thought "poor little orphan girl," but she remembered wishing she lived in the Baptist Home for Children. Those kids went to her school. Dressed nice. Ate the school lunches. Maybe they didn't have families, but it seemed she didn't either. Her father was almost always gone, home once in a blue moon to hand her mother a few dollars. Glory and four other children slept in one room; their mother held down two jobs.

She remembered one particular Thanksgiving.

FROM HER DESK in the fifth-grade classroom, Glory could smell the turkey cooking in the cafeteria. On the day before the holiday, the school served turkey with all the trimmings—dressing, mashed potatoes and gravy, rolls, and best of all, strawberry shortcake piled with whipped cream.

Glory tried to concentrate on what the teacher was writing on the blackboard, but hunger gnawed, her breakfast long gone. Beside her sat one of the girls from the home. She wore a clean starched dress every day, made A's in all her subjects, bragged about how the home would send her to college when she graduated from high school. Glory thought about college as she did about the moon—something only to imagine.

Finally the teacher set down her chalk. "Line up for lunch, children," she commanded.

Everyone but Glory scrambled to get in line. She stayed in her seat, and reached under her desk to pull out a brown paper bag. She stuffed it under her sweater and went to the back of the line. The teacher led them out the door.

That morning, as usual, Glory's mother had handed each of her children a sack lunch and a nickel to buy a carton of milk. She refused to accept the welfare lunches. "You take something free, you pay double in the end," she always said.

The students marched down the hallway toward the cafeteria.

When the teacher had rounded a corner, Glory slunk out a door to the playground. She scouted around to see that no one was looking, then stepped behind some azalea bushes that grew against a wall. She sat down, opened the sack, and unwrapped her food.

A thick slab of fatback lay between two pieces of cornbread. Two vanilla wafers. The food was hard to swallow without milk, but at least she didn't have to stare at those mounds of whipped cream.

GLORY WATCHED KITTY suck at one of her fingers, as if soothing it after jabbing it on a fork in the soapy water. For a moment, Glory felt pity for her. But she caught herself. No, she thought: That girl been cushioned from the real world all her life. Let her learn about the real world. I had to.

THE POOL HALL was not the kind of place Cappy and Jubal were used to back on Water Street in Wilmington. The tables looked new, the brushed felt was unworn, no cigarette burns or beer rings on the rails. Blues Traveler played on the jukebox, not too loud, and along the walls were a few video games; in one corner was an automated teller machine. A No Smoking sign hung above the bar, which did sell beer, but also cappuccino and fruit juices. At the pool tables were mostly men, with a few women, casually but neatly dressed.

"This don't look like hoochie-coochie people to me," Cappy said.

"Bet there ain't a hawkbill knife in the whole place," Jubal said. Standing around a pool table in a far corner, not mingling with the people playing billiards, were a dozen young men of high school age. Their hair was clipped short, and their shirttails were tucked in. The boys leaned in toward the table, poised, it seemed, for danger. Suddenly someone shouted, and they all leaped backward, erupting with laughter and catcalls.

"Let's check it out," Cappy said. As he and Jubal approached, a space opened in the group and they could see what was causing the commotion. On the table sat a gallon jar, the lid punched with air holes. Inside the jar buzzed a three-foot-long western rattlesnake. Thin streams of venom ran down the inside walls where the coiled rattler had struck.

Jubal knew the game. You put a fresh mean poisonous snake inside a large jar, then bet people they couldn't keep both hands on the outside of the glass when the serpent struck. After someone's hands were clasped against the glass for several seconds, the snake would sense the heat and lunge. The vast majority of people jerked back. Jubal doubted even he could make his hands stay in place.

"Looks like you're in your element, boy," Cappy said.

Jubal pushed his way to the edge of the table. A man wearing an apron with the pool hall's logo seemed to be the master of ceremonies. Jubal studied the snake. Blood was smeared on its snout; it must have broken a fang against the glass.

"You want to try your luck, Mister?" the man said. "Five dollars to ten you can't keep your hands on the glass."

Jubal looked back at Cappy, then stepped closer to the table and placed each of his hands beside the jar.

"You have to lay five dollars down first," the man said.

In response, Jubal grasped the neck of the jar with one hand and twisted the lid off with the other. The lid rattled onto the table, then to the floor. Jubal flipped the jar over and emptied the rattler on the table. The man and the boys gasped and reeled back.

The rattler was tired from all the harassment; Jubal grabbed it behind the head before it had time to coil. He lifted it writhing and dangling from his hand.

More gasps, and profanity, rose from the onlookers. "You crazy or something?" the man in the apron shouted.

Jubal dropped the rattler back into the jar, then picked the lid up from the floor and screwed it back on. He turned toward the group of boys, who stared intently at him. "Any of you from the academy?"

Several of the boys nodded.

"Which one of you is the gang leader?"

The boys glanced at one another. One nudged a tall freckled boy. The boy hesitantly raised his hand. "Sir, I'm the senior class president."

"Good. Pleased to meet you. I'm Jubal Lee, and that's the Captain. Let me buy you a fruit drink while we talk a little business."

JUBAL DROVE THE LAST STAKE into the ground with a flourish, pounding at the piece of wood until the top was even with the grass. He adjusted the guy rope, then stepped back from the brightly decorated tent. Cappy had bought it as drab canvas from a military surplus store in Wilmington, and Jubal had painted it before they went on the road. He dropped the sledgehammer and smiled, admiring his art.

At the bottom of the tent, tangled green vines covered the ground; they wound around tree trunks and stumps and logs. At the top, a shady canopy woven with branches and leaves spread like a great umbrella. Small creatures lived amid the jungle foliage, frogs and salamanders and snakes. A gnarled tree trunk, deeply rooted in the earth, rose to the sky and became a naked woman. Her arms spread wide in welcome, her breasts heavy, with erect nipples as red as rubies. Her hair was long and jet-black, her eyes green. Her lips were parted slightly, and in the corner of her mouth, the tip of her tongue was pink and forked like a serpent's.

"What do you think?" Jubal asked. Cappy, Glory, and Kitty stood with him before the entrance to the tent.

"You better paint some orchids over those tits," Cappy said. "Liable to get us thrown in jail."

"Is that supposed to be me?" Glory asked, her face brightened by a smile. "I don't have no forked tongue."

Jubal hunched one shoulder. "Let's say she's the embodiment of the show: virginal innocence bred with the carnal knowledge of the serpent."

"I didn't know you could paint this good," Glory said.

"I took a couple of art classes. I was always good at drawing."

"I didn't know you could talk so good," Cappy said. "Virginal innocence, shit! Some Barney Fife type is gonna put us all *under* the jail without a shovel."

EARLIER THAT MORNING, Cappy had paid the campground owner fifty dollars to allow them to have the show; he promised him a quarter of everything they took in. The only other camper on the grounds was off in a corner. Cappy hadn't even seen him, and wondered whether he'd show up.

Cappy and Jubal set up the stage and built benches of planks and cinder blocks. Out of plywood they made a box that looked like an upended coffin, and on the front, Jubal painted a voluptuous nude who vaguely resembled Glory. A six-inch hole was cut through the wood at the woman's crotch.

"I haven't seen one of these since I was fifteen," Jubal said. "Back when they had strip shows at the county fair."

"I don't know if these preppie boys will go for it or not," Cappy said. "Hell, they can turn on cable TV and see everything they want."

"Not from six inches away," Jubal said. "And they can't put their hands on it. I remember it was a thrill that time I went."

Glory surveyed the work from a few yards away. "I ought to knock you on your butt, drawing my hips that big," she told Jubal. "I ain't that big. Already got me with a forked tongue on the front of that tent."

Kitty walked over from where she'd been preparing lunch. She stared at the box. "What is that?"

"You don't want to know." Cappy shook his head. "We're gonna end up in jail. I got a bad feeling."

"This might be your night of initiation into the big time." Jubal grinned. "Don't even have to dance to be the star of this attraction."

"No!" Glory said. "Ain't but one star in this show. Miss Kitty too pure. She like prime rib more than hamburger."

Kitty looked at Glory. "What is this thing?" she asked again.

"You don't want to know," Cappy repeated. "You're the driver and the cook. We shouldn't have let you on the stage, even one time. Better to be ignorant and innocent."

"Lunch is ready," Kitty said. "Miss Darlene is already at the table. We need to eat. There are flies everywhere."

"Let's go," Glory said. "I ain't having seconds behind a fly. Ain't nothing nastier than a fly, unless it's that woman Jubal just painted. Those ain't my legs. I ought to knock you out, Jubal."

AT A LITTLE PAST EIGHT that night, a stream of cars entered the campground, each vehicle packed with prep school boys. Cappy played parking lot attendant, and assembled the boys before leading them to the tent.

The sixty-one boys in attendance were all well-groomed, and for the most part polite. The youngest looked no older than fourteen, the oldest no more than eighteen. Despite their appearance, they were not entirely innocent and wholesome. Cappy could smell beer and marijuana, and at least half of them were smoking cigarettes.

"Listen up, fellows," Cappy shouted. "This is a professional show, and I expect you to act like gentlemen. Admission is ten dollars a head, and for that you get to see a man, a woman, and a snake. It's the oldest act in history. You won't be disappointed." He scanned the boys' faces. No grumbling, no complaint about the price of admission. He immediately wished he had asked for fifteen. "After the main show, there's an additional attraction, for another small admission. Also, there are beverages on sale. For those of you who are eighteen, I'm of the old school. If a man is old enough to serve in the military, he's old enough to drink a cold beer. As far as who's driving, that's your business. Understand?"

A murmur of excitement rolled through the crowd. "Form a line," Cappy ordered.

The boys complied, hands going for their wallets. As disciplined as they appeared, even more apparent was their readiness to shed some discipline; laughter and comments leaked from their mouths; they gawked at the painting of the woman on the tent.

"Hell, this better be good for ten bucks," one boy said. "I can call up naked women on the Internet."

Cappy busied himself collecting money. Inside the tent, Kitty showed the boys to several long benches.

Darlene sat at a card table, beside a cooler filled with iced cans of soda and beer. On the table were bags of potato chips. A few of the taller boys walked straight from the entrance to Darlene's table.

"I need to see your driver's license," Darlene told the first boy in line. She took the boy's license, then held it close to her eyes. "All right. What do you need?"

"Five beers and five bags of potato chips," he said politely.

"You're sort of thirsty, aren't you?"

"Yes ma'am."

The boy gathered his purchases and walked to the benches, where he distributed the beers and chips. Many of the boys in the line did the same thing, and the tent was soon filled with the sounds of cans popping and bags crinkling.

Behind the curtain, Glory studied the crowd, deciding how brazen she should be, how much to show and how much to leave to the imagination—and thereby draw more boys to the special attraction after the main show.

"What did you want to see when you were that age?" she asked Jubal.

He was silent for a moment. "I wanted to see a king mackerel yanking at my fishing rod."

"That the only rod you were thinking about?"

"Just about."

"You were a late bloomer."

"No, it was a different world."

Jubal put a cassette into the tape player to give the boys some music to settle down with. When Cappy finished at the entrance, he waited until the boys seemed comfortable before stepping to the microphone.

"Gentlemen," he began. "Now, direct to you from the bayou country of Louisiana, raised in the swampland, with the face of an angel and a body sculpted by Satan himself, Miss Gloria Peacock, who will treat you and tempt you with her serpentine ways."

Cappy hit the switch that cut off the bare light bulb strung above the benches. With another flick, he turned on a blue floodlight over the stage. Kitty pulled the cord that drew the curtains apart. Glory, wearing a ripped sundress, bowed at center stage. The first notes of "Little Egypt" began, and she rolled her hips and raised herself. Wrapped around her neck was the newly molted corn snake. She didn't usually dance with live snakes, but for this audience she'd decided to go all-out. She slowly undressed to the music, and unwound the snake from her neck and rubbed her breasts with its smooth body. Several boys began shouting. At the end of the number, most of them were standing and clapping.

Between numbers, Cappy allowed time for more sales. Cans and bags littered the ground. As the third song ended, the boys were hooting and cheering: Glory lay on the floor in a G-string, scissoring her legs, the corn snake around one ankle, a king snake around the other. The curtains closed, to boisterous applause.

Cappy now introduced the next act. "Gentlemen, Glory's half brother, a ragin' Cajun. He sips rattlesnake venom like mother's milk. Jubal Lee!"

The curtains opened, the blue floodlight was replaced by a single red spotlight. Jubal, in cut-off jeans, skin glistening with baby oil, crouched in front of the coiled rattler. The noise that had accompanied Glory's performance was gone. The boys' eyes were wide as they watched.

"Man, I must be tripping!" one of them shouted.

"I *am* tripping!" another boy answered.

Jubal maneuvered within the strike zone on his first attempt, but he hesitated, not wanting to end his act so soon. The rattler had grown complacent in captivity, no longer the fireball it had been when fresh out of the swamp. By taunting with his decoy hand, Jubal got the serpent to strike twice, and he easily dodged the two blows. Finally he seized the rattler behind the head and stood, raising the serpent to eye level; its tail touched the floor. Jubal stepped forward and off the stage to within arm's length of the front row of the audience. The boys closest to him leaned back. Jubal tucked the rattler's tail between his knees, then reached and took a beer can out of the hand of the boy nearest him. He positioned the snake's head above the mouth of the can, then squeezed the venom glands. Twin streams of poison squirted into the can. He raised the vessel and drank, then handed it back to the stunned boy.

Glory came on for her final number, and had just begun when she felt cramps in her lower belly. She went on with the dance, though, a five-foot-long boa constrictor draped around her neck. Toward the end of the number, she was gritting her teeth. She felt dizzy; cold sweat trickled down her face. She finished the act lying facedown on stage, the serpent between her legs.

She stood for the boys' applause and attempted a smile. One boy climbed on his bench and tipped his beer can; liquid coursed down the sides of his mouth. His schoolmates shouted their encouragement. Glory turned away, her face contorted with pain. She handed the boa to Jubal and ducked out the rear of the tent. On her knees in the grass, she heaved her stomach's contents.

Glory felt a hand on her back, then the soft fold of a blanket being draped over her. She looked over her shoulder to see Kitty and Jubal.

"What's wrong?" Jubal asked. "You okay?"

Saliva hung from Glory's lip. "I'm sicker than a dog. Got cramps like a vise."

Cries for an encore rang from inside the tent, and then Cappy's voice above them. "Floor show is over, boys. Those of you brave enough, we got an extra treat for a small additional fee. Line starts here."

Kitty knelt beside Glory. "Maybe you have the flu."

Glory wiped her mouth with her hand. "More like spoiled Spam. I thought it tasted a little funny. Musta been them flies. Kitty, you ought to know you don't leave food out around flies."

She tried to stand, but her head spun rapidly, and she dropped back to her elbows. "God, I'm sick. I'm sick to the bone. Get me a cold rag, Jubal. Some ice to suck on."

"Maybe you have food poisoning," Kitty said. "We need to get you to a hospital."

"I wouldn't have it if you hadn't left the food out." Glory spit on the ground. "I be all right. Got to be. Them boys lining up for the tickle box right now." She rolled from her elbows to sit up. Tears streaked her makeup. "I got to get in the tickle box. We need that money."

"What's the tickle box?"

"White girl, you need to put two and two together."

"I've never heard of a tickle box."

"That box out there with the ugly picture Jubal painted, and the hole. What you think a tickle box is?"

"Ohhhh."

"Oh, yeah, and I got to get in there."

Glory tried to stand again, but got only to her knees. She fell back down, a sob bursting through her lips.

Jubal arrived with a washcloth and a bag of ice. Cappy followed him. "What's wrong, Glory?" he asked.

"Musta been that sandwich I ate before the show. I sick as a dog, Cap. Y'all gonna have to prop me up in the tickle box."

Jubal assembled an ice pack and pressed it to Glory's forehead.

"We'll cancel the tickle box," Cappy said.

"No we won't. All that money lost." Glory got to her feet. She swayed, then grabbed Jubal's arm to keep from going down. She leaned over and heaved again. "Oh, my belly hurts."

"That's it," Cappy said. "I'm sending them boys home."

"We need the money, Cap," Glory said between sobs.

"You can't stand up. Darlene can't do it, and I don't hear Kitty volunteering. I don't know of any extra vaginas around here."

Kitty's face turned to the ground.

"Hell, I wouldn't let you do it anyway," Cappy growled. "I'm sending them home."

"There *is* a way," Glory said. "There's a way if Jubal is man enough."

"Oh, shit," Jubal said.

"After all," Glory went on, "what's inside that dark hole is all in them boys' minds."

JUBAL AND KITTY helped Glory to the bus, then returned to escort Darlene. Cappy stalled for time, pacifying the crowd by selling them more beer. After fifteen minutes, he told the boys to line up.

"She's so hot we have to put her in a box," he shouted over the restless audience. "Otherwise, you might go blind. Five dollars gets you a peak and a sneak. You get to eyeball that thing, then a quick little pet before it bites you."

All but two boys had lined up, money in hand. The two who didn't join in staggered outside, retching from too much beer.

"A peek and a sneak," Cappy repeated. "Don't look but a second, or you might go blind. Sneak your arm in there and cop a feel—only a second or two, or your fingers will burn."

Cappy took a five-dollar bill from the first boy in line. The boy peered over his shoulder at his schoolmates, then bent and looked into the hole. A dim blue light illuminated a torso, a belly covered by a short white teddy, garter belt supporting white sheer stockings. No panties, a bush of pubic hair visible. The faint light muted the features; this was a nude done in pastels.

"Don't look too long," Cappy said. "It's like an eclipse." He tapped the boy on the shoulder. The boy looked back openmouthed at his friends.

"God almighty," he exclaimed.

"Don't burn your fingers," Cappy warned. "This ain't the fucking Internet."

The boy hesitated, then slowly inserted his hand into the hole. He jerked back when he first touched flesh, but a smile spread across his face as he stroked pubic hair. "Hey," he said, "this is the real thing."

"Time." Cappy hit the boy's arm lightly. "You don't want to draw back a nub."

INSIDE THE TICKLE BOX, Jubal tried to separate himself from what was happening. The boys made him think of his own youth, and he recalled a day in junior high. He was in the seventh grade and small for his age; the growth spurt that pushed his height to more than six feet wouldn't come until ninth grade.

The day before, Johnny Reinhardt had beaten him up again, bloodying his lip and making him fall and skin an elbow. Andy, Jubal's older brother, was in high school now, and Jubal had to fend for himself.

"Bunch of no-'count fishing people." Johnny smirked, standing above Jubal. "Your mama smells like a mullet."

"If Andy was here, you wouldn't say that." Jubal blinked back tears.

"Awww, I'd kick his butt too. Big brother is gone, sucker. So get used to it. I'm gonna kick your ass, every day.

The Reinhardts were considered white trash by most people, Jubal knew. Johnny's father was laid up drunk most of the time. None of the children looked alike, but they all were bullies.

The next day Jubal brought a bag with a fat banded water snake to school—he knew how closely that species resembled the poisonous cottonmouth. He hid the bag in his desk and at the end of the day transferred the bag to his jacket pocket. Outside on the school grounds, just as Jubal had wanted, Johnny approached with several friends. Jubal untied the bag and pulled out the snake. "Cottonmouth," he said. "A fat one."

Johnny stepped backward. When Jubal advanced with the snake, Johnny took another step back, then tripped. In an instant, Jubal was on him, one knee on his chest, the snake close to his face.

"Mess with me now!" Jubal screamed. "This snake is deadly, and I'm going to shove it down your throat."

The water snake struggled, then gaped and emptied its bowels on Johnny's chest. He shrieked and began crying.

"You ever mess with me again," Jubal warned, "and I'll put rattlesnakes in your house."

A teacher separated the boys and ordered Jubal to take his snake home. He got a paddling from the principal, but Johnny and every other bully left him alone after that. He felt like Moses with the Red Sea rolling back.

WHEN THE BOY'S FINGERS first touched him, a shiver rolled up Jubal's spine—a reaction as primal as a rattler's bite. He breathed deeply and clamped his legs tighter together, further protecting his genitals between his thighs. He thought of his snakes, and when the second boy touched him, Jubal did not flinch. It's all in the mind, he told himself.

About ten seconds for each boy, Jubal calculated. And there were about sixty boys. A little less than ten minutes and the ordeal would be over, and they'd make another three hundred dollars or so. He could eat a T-bone steak tonight instead of Spam. With the money they'd earned here, maybe they could ride straight to Oregon and Miss Darlene's land.

Jubal had counted forty-five gropers when he heard the slow wail of a siren.

Cappy cursed and banged on the box. "It's the heat, Jubal! Get out of there."

Jubal freed himself from the box and ran for the tent. He crawled underneath, then sprang to his feet in the cool night air.

L ooks like somebody's been having some fun." A tall, thin man in uniform walked through the tent, kicking empty beer cans out of his way. The terrified boys, eyes fixed on his sheriff's badge, remained in their seats; a lone aging man was on the stage. The sheriff was followed by a pimply-faced younger man, his deputy. Near the stage, the sheriff picked up a spangled bra by one strap, sniffed it, and dropped it to the floor.

"Looks like you boys been having a good ol' time." He looked suspiciously at a group of sealed buckets on the stage, and tapped one lightly with his boot. There was a buzzing inside. "That's not a time bomb, is it?"

"No sir," Cappy said.

"What is it?"

"A rattlesnake."

"I'll take your word for it." The sheriff walked to the painted box, stared at the naked lady, then leaned and peered into the hole. "Damn! Melton," he addressed his companion, "you know what this place is?"

"I have an idea, sir."

"Hell, you're too young. What we have here is a old-fashioned traveling hoochie-coochie snake show. I haven't seen one in twenty years." The sheriff pointed at the painted box. "You got any idea what that is?"

The deputy shook his head.

"The carnival used to have these when I was a boy. We called it a feel-good box. It did too."

The sheriff took his time searching the faces of the boys. Each one dropped his eyes from the man's gaze.

"You know, I could take all you boys in. Impound your cars too. Every one of you would get kicked out of school."

One of the younger boys was sniffling, on the verge of tears.

"But this town needs your dollars. It needs your mamas and daddies rolling in here with big bucks at graduation." The sheriff crushed a beer can with his heel. "Personally, I'm kinda proud of you. I always took you fellows to be a bunch of wussies." The sheriff pointed to the box. "You know, boys, you ought to remember this night. You're seeing the last of a breed here, a simpler time gone by. I thought it was gone already."

His faced hardened. "You boys get out of here. I've got your license numbers. You run a red light, and I'll personally see that you're punished. Go on, get!"

The boys stood frozen, then started in a mass for the tent door. Cappy was edging toward the door himself when the sheriff called to him.

"Not you, pop." The sheriff told the deputy to search him.

Cappy lifted his arms while the deputy patted him down.

"You have any weapons on you?" the sheriff asked.

"Only a pocketknife."

"Empty your pockets."

Cappy sighed, then reached into his trousers and pulled out a thick roll of bills. The deputy took the money and handed it to the sheriff, who slowly counted it.

The sheriff whistled. "More than a thousand dollars. You must have a class show." He walked to the ice chest and took out one of the few remaining cold beers, popped the top, and sat down on a bench. "You want a beer?" he asked Cappy.

"I could use one."

The sheriff nodded toward the cooler. "Don't drink all the evidence."

Cappy fished out a beer for himself and sat down across from the sheriff.

"Where's your crew?"

"I'm working alone."

"I suppose you were wearing that bra over there? And you were in the feel-good box too? Hell, Mister, those boys are dumber than shit, but they ain't blind."

The sheriff noted Cappy's tattoos. "Looks like you were in the military."

"Army, thirty years."

"Enlisted?"

"For the first ten years I was. I got a field commission. Retired as a captain."

"Can you prove it?"

Cappy took his retirement ID from his wallet and handed it to the sheriff. The sheriff read the card and gave it back.

"You pull a tour in 'Nam?"

"Three, back to back."

"I was there in 'sixty-six. First Cavalry Division."

Cappy knew that what they had been doing was illegal, that if the sheriff wanted to, he could arrest everyone and impound the bus. "Sheriff, you have my money. What do you say I'm packed and out of here in two hours. I'll drive straight to the state line."

"Captain, you know I can't do that. You've broken the law. I'm paid to uphold the law." The sheriff finished his beer and turned to his deputy. "Melton, go to the cruiser and do a radio check."

"Yes sir." The deputy exited the tent.

"Look, Captain," the sheriff said, "I know you have people with you. I know you have a woman with you who could fill out that bra. I could make a lot of trouble, but I'm not going to. A mustang captain that pulled three tours in 'Nam can't be all bad. I'm gonna confiscate nothing but this money. I'll ask the magistrate to set a low bail. If you get out and bolt, that's not my business. The courts are too full, anyway."

Cappy nodded. "Under the circumstances, that's reasonable. But I still wish you'd let me slide out of here. You said it yourself—this place ain't no harm. Boys their age are getting murdered in the streets."

"I know it. Off the record, I'd feel safer with them being here than doing what goes on in their dorm rooms. But I have a job to do. My deputy looks up to me." The sheriff stood. "Now, Captain, I've got to read you your rights and put some cuffs on you. That's all formality, nothing personal. As a captain, you know rules are what makes the world work."

FROM A WINDOW of the darkened bus, everyone watched as Cappy got into the squad car and was taken away.

"Oh, Lord. We're sunk now," Jubal said.

"You best be thanking the Lord you got away. Wouldn't you be a pretty sight in the lockup." Glory was feeling better now, well enough to tease Jubal.

He fumbled at his costume. He rolled the garter belt and pulled off the stockings. "I wouldn't have been taken alive in this." Under cover of a blanket, he slipped his jeans on. "I'll go to the police station and see what the charges are. Maybe I can bail him out."

"With what?" Glory asked. "Cap was holding all the money. Bet he ain't got a nickel now."

"Well, I have to try. We've got to get to Denver on time."

"Let the girl go," Darlene said.

"Kitty doesn't know anything about jails," Jubal replied. "I've got to figure out a way to get him out."

"Let her go. They can't charge her with anything. You're pushing your luck."

"Darlene's right," Glory said. "There's 'bout fifty boys in this town that can identify your face and your crotch."

"Shut up, Glory. I did what I had to do."

"You did good. Them boys probably whacking off right now, thinking how lovely you were. Like I say, it all in the mind."

"Let the girl go," Darlene repeated. "That sheriff's not a bad man, else we'd all be downtown right now."

"I'll walk over there." Jubal put on his shirt. "Makes me shiver to think of those boys out there. I'm taking a long shower as soon as I get back."

"It wasn't you they were touching, honey," Glory said. "They were thinking 'bout me."

"It damn sure felt like they were touching me."

Darlene stood up and walked close to Kitty. "That sheriff has a wound, Kitty. Touch him where he hurts. He's not a bad man."

"What you talking 'bout, Miss Darlene?" Glory asked.

"There's been enough touching around here for one day," Jubal said.

"Touch him where he hurts." Darlene rested a hand on Kitty's shoulder, her voice slow and thoughtful.

Glory squeezed her arms to her chest. "Miss Darlene, lately you saying things that scare me."

THE POLICE STATION was in the center of town, nearly a mile from the campground. Jubal coached Kitty as they walked there.

"Don't admit to anything. Just say you're a friend and you want to see what his bail is set at. Don't say you were ever in the tent."

The sheriff was at a desk counting change when Kitty entered. He looked up at her. "Are you having trouble, Miss?"

"No. No sir."

"Wait just a second, then, till I finish counting. I don't want to lose track."

The sheriff resumed his counting. On the desk were nearly a dozen jars, full of change and scattered dollar bills. Taped to each jar were a picture of a blonde girl and a label: "Please help Tammy

Spencer receive a bone marrow transplant. She will thank you with her life."

The sheriff scribbled on a sheet of paper. He pushed his chair back from the desk and looked again at Kitty. "Now, how can I help you?"

Kitty's stomach fluttered. "I've come to inquire about a man you might have in custody."

"Being that I have only one man in custody, I must assume you're from that bus."

"I'm a friend of Mr. Tucker's."

"A friend? You don't exactly look like you're with the show. At least the evidence I have wouldn't fit you."

"I'm not with the show."

"Is he your father?"

"No, just a friend. Sir, I was wondering if bail has been set."

"Yes."

"How much is it?"

"Miss, your captain friend broke several laws. I've gone easy with the charges, but the magistrate set bail at one thousand dollars."

"A thousand! We don't have that much."

"It's a thousand dollars, or he sits in jail for a couple of weeks till his case comes up. Then, I reckon, he'll get a small fine and time served."

"Sir, we can't wait two weeks. We have a sick woman with us."

"Don't talk to me about sickness." The sheriff rubbed his forehead, his eyes closed. "I could have been real hard on your friend. On all of you. But the magistrate set the bail. I can't change that."

Kitty looked again at the picture of the little girl on the jars. Her eyes went to the sheriff's name tag. The wrinkles in his forehead were as deep as knife wounds.

"Sir, can I ask a personal question?"

"Maybe."

"Is Tammy your daughter?"

"My granddaughter."

"I'm sorry."

"Hell, throw a quarter in the jar. That's about all most people will give. A school full of rich kids, have money for a traveling show, want to save the whales. But they can't spare a dollar."

"Excuse me." Kitty felt odd being so abrupt. "Is there a rest room I can use?"

The sheriff pointed.

Inside the rest room, Kitty pulled the roll of bills from her pocket. Thirteen left. She heard Darlene's voice: *Touch him where he hurts.*

Kitty rubbed the money between her fingers. She pulled out three bills, hesitated, then took two more. She replaced the roll in her pocket. When she returned to the office, the sheriff was counting through another pile of coins. Kitty laid the five hundred-dollar bills in front of him.

"I want to help."

The sheriff stared at the stack, then spread the bills like poker cards. "I can't take this. Hell, this is half your friend's bail."

"We don't have the other half. Might as well contribute to a good cause."

Kitty turned and walked to the door. She was closing it behind her when the sheriff spoke. "Stop. Come back here a minute."

Kitty walked back to the desk.

"Is this a bribe?"

"No. It's a gift."

The sheriff stroked his face from forehead to chin. "You know, there's not much crime in this town, so I'm pretty lax about security. I've got to go back there in the file room and do some work."

He gathered the bills and stuck them in his pocket. "I sort of wished tonight that I could have been a boy in the audience watching the show. Wished that I was sixteen, and danger was something that happened only on the stage, that you could look at and then walk away." He shook his head. "I know that ain't so. It surrounds us. Even little girls can get cancer."

The sheriff stood. "I'm leaving my keys on the desk. I don't check prisoners again until six a.m. A man breaks jail, he could be out of state before he was missed. I don't really worry about that, though. I thank you for your generosity."

Kitty watched the sheriff walk into another room and close the door. She stared at the keys on his desk. Did he mean what it sounded like? Or was he just setting her up—was he going to arrest her too?

She lifted the keys from the desk carefully, holding them with two fingertips as if they were hot. She stared at the door, afraid the sheriff would suddenly open it, gun drawn, and arrest her. Nothing happened. She jingled the keys. Nothing.

Kitty stepped quickly toward the cells. "Captain," she said softly, peering between the bars at the concrete floors and bare bunks and exposed urinals. Cappy sat on the bunk in the third cell, his head propped in his hands.

"Captain?"

He blinked as if he had been dozing, then stood.

"Captain, I've got the keys."

"What the hell!"

"We have to be fast. The sheriff is working in the file room."

Kitty tried to insert one key into the lock.

"You're fixing to get us shot! How'd you get those keys?"

"We don't have a lot of time to talk. Which one is it?"

"Damn, Kitty! You know I can't break out of jail. The FBI will be trailing me."

"Shhh. Don't shout. He wants you to go." Kitty tried another key.

"He said that?"

"Sort of." Finally a key slid into the lock. Kitty turned it and pulled the door open. "Come on."

"We're gonna get our asses shot!"

Kitty cracked the door to the sheriff's office and peeked in, then motioned Cappy forward. They tiptoed across the room, Kitty pausing to replace the keys on the desk. In another instant they were outside, running toward Jubal, who waited in the shadows.

THE BUS HAD TRAVELED more than fifty miles before Cappy stopped watching through the rear window for police lights behind them. He sat down with a beer, draining most of the can in one long draft.

"Now I can add fugitive to my résumé," he said. "They'll probably have a barricade waiting for me at the state line. I can't believe you did that, Kitty."

"I didn't know what else to do. He just left the keys there. I think he wanted you to go."

"She touched his wound," Darlene said.

"She must have touched more than his wound."

"Hush!" Glory scolded. "The Lord delivered you, Cap. Like Daniel from the lions' den."

"I wish he'd delivered my money too. That guy took a thousand dollars off me. I'm glad I stuffed a couple hundred in the other pocket."

"It was for a good cause," Kitty said.

"Good cause, my ass. Might buy a new stoplight. *If* the sheriff even turned the money in, which I doubt."

"You never know what that money might be used for."

"I know what it won't be used for. We better hope we strike pay dirt in Denver."

"Quit bitching, Cap," Jubal said. "At least you weren't violated like me. I never even got to take my shower."

"I owe you for that one," Glory said. "I owe you big time, honey. You got to believe what I do. They can touch your body, but they can't touch your soul. You did what you had to do, and your soul is clean. They can't touch that."

KITTY THOUGHT she was seeing clouds on the horizon, the dark mass of a front moving higher and higher. She drove through flat grasslands, past widely spaced ranches where silos loomed above herds of fatted Holstein and Angus. Occasionally she spied antelope grazing, hawks sitting watch on telephone poles, the black-and-white flashes of magpies.

"We might be headed for some rain," Kitty said.

Jubal looked at the horizon, whistling long and low. "I don't think rain. We might be in for a rock slide, though."

"What do you mean?"

Jubal grabbed the road atlas and flipped to the map of Colorado. "Yep," he announced. "That's the Rocky Mountains."

The mountains appeared even higher as the miles passed, gray and blue against the bright sky, a giant wall rising stark from the plains. Kitty could now distinguish individual shapes in the mass, craggy peaks topped with snow. The wall of rock was as starkly different from the flatlands as the ocean from the shoreline; it was the entry into another world.

She felt the excitement, a great bubble of joy. Her palms hardened to the steering wheel. Nearly a week now on the road, and more had happened in that brief time than in all her life before. She wished the bus could go faster and begin the climb into air that was cool and sweet and nearer to the sun.

"I never knew mountains were so beautiful," Kitty said. "They look so different when you're flying above them—I mean in movies they look so different."

"They're pretty," Jubal said. "But I want to see what's beyond them. See the ocean. Those rocks haven't changed one bit in ten thousand years. The ocean, it's different one minute to the next."

Cappy joined them at the front of the bus and looked through the windshield. "Big, aren't they. I never had no use for mountains. Too easy to get shot at when you're in them."

"Ain't nobody shooting at you now," Glory told him.

"Oh, there's always somebody gunning for you."

"How's Miss Darlene?"

"Not good," Cappy said in a low voice. "Not good at all. Though she won't tell me how bad she feels. We need to get her to a doctor."

"What's the game plan in Denver?" Jubal asked.

"More perverts, I reckon. All I have for them is a name and a phone number."

"We're lucky Kitty crawled under the bus," Glory said. "Even if she don't know shit about flies. Else your old ass still be in the slammer, Cap."

"I'd probably be safer there," Cappy answered. "The law has

rules. The world is going straight to hell. No discipline. Perversion everywhere."

"Don't get started," Glory said. "Soon you'll be foaming at the mouth again."

"Mile-High City, that's what they call Denver," Cappy continued. "Can't wait to see what this next group is like. Probably a mile high on dope's what they are. I ever see Jasper again, I'm slugging him square in the nose."

AGAINST THE NATURAL BACKDROP of the mountains, Denver stood vertical, its tall buildings glinting in the late-day sun. The gray haze of auto exhaust hung like a shroud and contrasted sharply with the snow on the highest peaks.

Jubal, who was now driving, had not expected so much concrete, steel, and glass. "We're ruining it all, aren't we? My first glimpse of the Rockies, and I see smog and skyscrapers. Makes me sick."

"They can't build on the mountains," Kitty said. "There's millions of acres beyond that ridge with nothing but animals and trees."

"They'll find a way to build on it." Jubal pointed through the windshield. "See that mountain over there? I read that some developer is building a restaurant on top of it. A restaurant that revolves. A cable car will take people up there. Millions of acres ain't much when there's so many people.

"I guess you never really thought of a place as home, Kitty. Being how you grew up."

"I have an idea what home is."

"When I was a kid, there wasn't a house within a mile of where I grew up. We had to drive five miles to the nearest supermarket. I bought my first bicycle with money I'd earned digging clams. They were everywhere. Now you couldn't find a peck if you hunted all day. Houses are everywhere. You're not even supposed to eat the clams because of the pollution. Goddamn developers."

"I'm sorry, Jubal."

"You ever hear of the Monroes? Naw, you wouldn't have heard of them. Anyway, they're this rich family in Wilmington. Own half the town. They ran us out of business. Stank up the water. Dried up the marshes so they could build condos. There's this island they own where me and my brother used to camp out. That's next on the list. Five years from now, there won't be a snake on it."

"What makes you think they're going to develop Boar Island?"

"How'd you know what I was talking about?"

"Well, I . . . I was guessing. The other day you mentioned Boar Island. What makes you think it's going to be developed?"

"The word's out. I know a man who runs a survey crew. Condos and retirees, within five years. The Monroes don't have souls. Just bank accounts."

Kitty pressed her thumbnail against her palm. "Maybe they're not all bad, Jubal."

"Who you kidding! A Monroe?"

Kitty shut her eyes. The sunlight was bright through her closed lids, as if she were staring at a blank movie screen. Pictures from deep within her mind began to unreel.

WILLIAM MONROE hit the button on the skiff's motor when they were several yards from the beach. The bow was carried high up on the sand. Cornelia, ten years old, hopped out. Her father, his face weathered like a slab of driftwood, his eyes still clear and blue, was slower getting out.

"It's like being in a foreign country, Dad." The girl called him that only when they were alone. Her mother insisted on the more formal title "Father."

"It's pretty near a foreign country, the way the mainland is changing. Ain't a road on the whole island."

They stood on a three-hundred-acre island in the mouth of the Cape Fear River. It was covered with scrub oak and pines, uninhabited but brimming with wildlife. Cornelia spied a sand dollar beside her bare foot. She bent and picked it up.

"Look, Dad. It's perfect."

"This whole place is perfect. Little Eden, I call it, 'cept the snakes can't talk."

Will Monroe took his daughter's hand and began to show her the island. At a sandbar on the southern side, he pointed at an oyster bed emerging as the tide dropped.

"Me and Herman Lee, back when we first started fishing together, used to anchor here sometimes and eat oysters by the gutful. Oysters big as your palm. We hocked everything, even our names, to get that first boat. I'd've probably stayed with fishing if he hadn't died." Will's eyes were shiny with recollection. "Probably would have stayed poor too. Sure wouldn't own this island."

"Who died, Dad?"

"Oh, just a man I used to be partners with. We'd been friends since grade school. Then two years after we bought our boat, he died in a car wreck. Left a wife, two kids. I couldn't fish alone, so I sold the boat and got my realtor's license."

"Did he have a daughter?"

"No, they were both boys."

"What happened to them?"

"I don't know. I should have kept up with them after Herman died, but I didn't. There's a lot I didn't do."

Cornelia saw her first live alligator that day, a ten-footer lying on a mudbank. She saw egrets, and heard the whistles and calls of birds in the trees. After a picnic lunch, she and her father went fishing. A run of spot began, and Cornelia caught her first fish.

Over the next few years, she visited the island frequently with her father. Will found a sense of peace there, not just an escape from the real estate business, and a link to a simpler, truer life. For Cornelia, the time with her father was a chance for love and affection without complications—something she lacked with her mother.

Her last visit to the island with her father came a week before she was to begin her freshman year at Cape Fear Academy. They were in a twin-engine inboard, fishing near a sandbar.

"Why do I have to go to a private school, Dad? I'd be a lot happier at Hoggard, and the tuition would be lower."

"If I had my say, you would go to Hoggard. But your mother has different views." William cast his line in a long arc across the water. "You know, baby, I hate what my life and your mother's have become. I hardly recognize myself now as a man who used to own a fishing trawler. I hardly have the time to go fishing."

"That's because you work too much. All those real estate deals, and Mother with all her social functions. Sometimes it seems that sending me to school is a way to get me out of the house as much as to give me an education."

"Don't say that, honey. Your mother loves you. I know we've

let money get too big a hold on our lives. If I could go back in time, I'd change some things."

Cornelia's fishing rod bent; she drew back on the pole to set the hook. Twenty seconds later, she pulled in a large flounder, to go in the cooler with several mullets and a few sea bass.

"I want you to bring your children out here someday," her father said. "This island, I don't want it developed. I'll probably have to fight to keep it, but I don't want it bulldozed and cut into lots like every other damn thing around here. I want you to be able to tell your children that their grandfather used to fish this sandbar with you."

Less than three years later, at the reading of her father's will, Cornelia was awarded a trust fund of half a million dollars, to be turned over to her on her twenty-first birthday, plus sole ownership of her father's fishing boat and the river island.

JUBAL FOLLOWED Cappy's instructions and took the beltway around the big city. After a phone call to their next host, Cappy had learned they were to proceed north, toward the smaller town of Loveland.

"Who's the contact this time, Cap?" Jubal asked.

"Woman named Calico Dove. Jasper put a star by her name. I bet she's a real bird."

"I like the name of her town," Glory said. "Maybe we won't get in a fistfight this time. Loveland. Sounds like my kind of place."

Loveland was more in the image of what Jubal had expected Colorado to be, a town nestled in a valley between steep mountains, the air clean and fragrant. To the west were the craggy peaks of

Rocky Mountain National Park, silent and awesome as time itself. Jubal drove the bus to a campground on the outskirts of town, where they set up for the night only yards from a clear rushing stream. The sun had already slipped beyond the mountains, but an hour of daylight was left when Jubal took a lightweight fishing rod and walked along the stream to where the water cascaded into a small circular pool. He baited a hook with a kernel of canned corn and cast into the middle of the pool. The line went taut and he reeled in a ten-inch rainbow trout. He lifted the fish against the coral sky and admired the flash of colors. Suddenly he felt pulled between blue-green aspens and sea oats, snow melt and saltwater, crisp chill air off ancient glaciers and high haze along a balmy coast.

BRIGHT SUN SPARKLED on the water, and a light wind blew out of the west. The two young men, enjoying a rare day without paying customers, were on their second or third beers. With several red snappers already in the ice chest, their trolling lines were out, the motor set low, as they cruised through the water.

"I can't believe you quit," Jubal told his brother. "A four-year baseball scholarship at ECU. Hell, the Braves were scouting you!"

The corners of Andy's mouth broke into wrinkles as he smiled. "And leave this? I was born on the water, remember."

"You were born on the water because the boat got caught on a shoal when Ma went into labor. You were born to hurl a fastball."

Andy raised his beer and gulped. He lowered the can and wiped his mouth. "I've got it figured out. I'll still play summers with Triple A. My fastball is still a baby. I get my skipper's license, then

I'll give Atlanta a call. If that doesn't pan out, I've got the water. The water will always be there. My pitching arm won't."

Jubal stared at the deck. "Well, if that makes you happy. I guess you're right. Dreams mean more than money. I didn't think I'd make it through the first year of school, but I did. Had a three-O. I'm going to finish."

"I'll kick your ass if you don't. Imagine, a Lee with a college degree. You ought to leave those damn snakes alone, though. Rattlers don't respect education."

Jubal raised his hand and stared at it, then clenched his fist. "They respect this hand. The hand is quicker than the rattlesnake. That's a law. I'm quicker than a rattlesnake, and you're quicker than the batter, and we're both going to end up ahead of the count."

Andy grasped Jubal's hand. "Deal, little brother." As they dropped hands, the fishing line began to sing. The rod bent, the line stripping out as the fish ran.

"Whew," Andy breathed. "That ain't no red snapper. I hope the line holds."

Half an hour passed before the big marlin tired and Andy could reel it in. His face dripped with sweat, and his thick arms were drawn tight. "Bet she's over five hundred pounds," he said slowly. "Throttle down and bring us portside. Get the gaff ready."

Jubal steered the boat left and shifted into neutral. From the stow box, he lifted a three-pronged hook that was tied to about ten feet of rope. Standing portside, he stared at the dark shape of the fish in the water. "God, it's a monster."

A powerboat sped by, too close, crowding them. A bikini-clad girl waved from her perch on the bow. Andy held the fishing pole high as he brought the marlin in near the boat. He unbuckled his harness with one hand, then stood and raised the pole even higher to bring the fish to the surface. The marlin's head broke the water first, one flat black eye glittering cold in the sun. Jubal, rope coiled in one hand, gaff poised in the other, stood above the fish. When the pole was nearly vertical, the fish lying on its side, Andy gave the word: "Stick him!"

Jubal struck downward, driving one prong of the gaff deep into the marlin's back. Wake from the powerboat smacked their craft broadside, and Jubal toppled backward, knocking Andy down. Jubal dropped the rope, stumbled, and fell against the console; his head knocked the gear into forward. Immediately the boat lurched.

The accident happened in seconds, but in Jubal's memory time was stretched into thin threads of eternity. The gaff rope had fallen in coils around Andy's feet. He dived for the fishing pole, now sliding over the side of the boat. As the rope played out with the departing fish, a crude knot tightened around Andy's bare right foot, and he was forced to the deck and toward the stern. He rolled to his belly and his eyes met Jubal's.

"Cut the throttle!" Andy slammed into the stern, where he braced with his legs before the weight of the fish dragged him up and over the bulkhead. Jubal hit the engine kill button and lunged toward his brother; he locked his hands around Andy's shoulders just before he was pulled over the side. A ringing silence engulfed the two brothers as they looked into each other's eyes. Bright sun sparkled on the water as before, and a dying marlin drifted slowly toward his grave in the deep water. . . .

TWICE MORE Jubal cast, and twice more he reeled in a rainbow trout. He exhaled deeply, trying to clear his lungs of salt air and sea spray. He heard footsteps behind him, and turned to see Kitty climbing down the rocks.

"You mind if I watch?" she asked.

"No."

"I remember fishing when I was younger." She sat on a boulder, pulled her knees to her chest and hugged them. "It's getting chilly."

Jubal didn't answer. He baited his hook again, cast, reeled in another trout.

"You're really good."

"Not much sport here. It's like fishing in a bucket. But we can use the food."

Kitty rested her chin on her knees. "What would you do with Boar Island if you owned it, Jubal?"

"I can't answer that. I don't own it, and never will. I ain't exactly one of the Monroes."

"What if you were? Just pretend you were rich and owned the island. Wouldn't you want to have all that money?"

"Money? I've never had much, so I don't know what I'm missing. I'd just leave the place alone. Maybe build me a little cabin on the south side."

"What else? What's your dream?"

"Shit, Kitty. I don't believe much in dreams."

"Come on, just pretend."

Jubal smiled reflectively. "I'd get me a degree in marine biology.

Hell, maybe a Ph.D. I'd turn that whole island into a preserve." His smile broadened. "I'd build a camp there for kids to come to—not just any kids but poor kids—and I'd show them how to dig clams and fish and run around like wild Indians like me and my brother did. There would be no electricity. I'd put a cannon onshore, and if some rich kids on ski boats got within a hundred yards, I'd fire once, over them, and if they didn't leave, I'd blow them out of the water."

Kitty laughed. "Would you hire me? I could be the cook."

"Maybe. After you went to culinary school."

"Would you hire your brother? He could be in charge of the wild Indians."

Jubal's smile went flat, and he turned away. "I can't. He's dead."

Kitty straightened her legs, then stood. "I . . . I'm sorry, Jubal. I didn't know."

"Well, he is, and I ain't rich, and never will be. Boar Island is dead too, or soon will be. I've got about as many dreams right now as these fish do."

The line trembled again, then went taut. Jubal pulled back on the pole and set the hook. The fish surfaced and tail-walked across the water. The morsel of corn that had lured it to its death gleamed like a nugget of gold.

THE OIL SIZZLED when Glory dropped in a pinch of cornmeal, and smoke rose from the frying pan. "Me and Kitty can get on with the cooking as soon as Mr. Jubal Lee gets over here and cuts the damn heads off these fishes."

"You're supposed to leave the heads on trout," Jubal said.

"Not me. No sir. I ain't eating nothing looking back at me."

Ten trout lay on a paper plate, freshly scaled and gutted, their rainbow colors catching the light from the lantern.

"People in Europe always eat fish with the head on," Kitty said. "It's called *poisson complet*."

"Well, this ain't Europe, Miss Smarty. Fancy talk for some little orphan ain't never been close to Europe. Come on, Jubal. I'm tired and hungry, and I ain't eating no fish heads."

Grinning, Jubal unfolded his knife and sliced into the first trout.

"Bury it with some seed corn or something," Glory continued. "Be like Pocahontas. People didn't evolve from the jungle to eat damn fish heads."

Glory took a headless fish from Jubal and showed Kitty how to coat it with cornmeal before putting it into the oil.

At the edge of the light, Darlene sat in a lawn chair with a blanket draped over her. Cappy, in another chair beside her, held out a cup half filled with beer. He had to touch her hand with the rim before she took it.

"You ain't seeing so good, are you?" Cappy asked.

"I'm seeing all right. I'm seeing things I never thought I'd see."

"You need to be in a hospital."

Darlene sipped from her cup. "No I don't. That wouldn't do any good. I need to be here with you. I need to be on my land. When the time is right, I need you to make me an honest woman."

"You weren't never close to honest, Darlene."

"I wasn't ever close to dying either."

"You're not close to dying."

"I see things in my head, but I don't see me. There's just a blackness. I want to be honest for one time in my life."

"Hell, Darlene, I'd a married you years ago if you'd asked."

"I wanted *you* to ask."

"I didn't think I deserved you."

"You didn't. But you could have asked. I would have lowered my standards."

"There's a lot in this life I didn't do." Cappy's voice was low and hollow.

"I keep dreaming of you falling. But you're smiling as you fall."

"You're just having nightmares," Cappy said. "Medicine always makes me dream crazy."

"I'm also worried about Jubal. He's given up. Keeps grabbing the biggest snakes he can find. He doesn't have to milk big snakes. He could use a chicken snake and nobody would know the difference."

"I'm worried about him too. He's young and reckless, but there's more to it."

"I dreamed about his hand last night. It was on fire, and he was just standing there looking at it and laughing."

"That beer is starting to talk through you now." Cappy extended his hand. "Come on to the table. That fish smells good."

THEY FEASTED ON TROUT, down to the bones, even the crisp tails, and cole slaw and fried cornmeal patties.

Jubal's chin was shiny with grease. "Man, you're making me homesick," he said. "I haven't eaten this good in so long."

"I prefer saltwater fish, but this ain't bad, Glory," Cappy said.

"Don't compliment me. Kitty did the cooking."

"And she did all right." Cappy packed his mouth with more cornbread.

Kitty smiled. "Don't thank me. Jubal caught the fish."

"Just thank the Lord," Glory said. "We eating manna from heaven."

Cappy patted his stomach. "I spoke to that Dove woman again. She wants us ready to go at seven tomorrow night."

"What's her pleasure?" Jubal asked.

"Lord knows. She talked like a Harvard graduate. She said she'd heard all about us."

"I hope she into straight sin and degradation," Glory said, "and not like that pervert Reginald."

While the others had settled down for the night, Kitty sat by the lantern writing a postcard. "Dear Esther," she began, "Tonight I ate fresh trout that I cooked myself. I am feeling a fullness inside that is not just from the food. . . ."

ONE LONG, SLOW BREATH after another, Cappy filled his air mattress. He had brought his bed close to the stream, where the dancing water was like music. He would sleep well tonight, tired from the previous night's quick departure. The mountain air was chilly; his urine steamed when he relieved himself on a rock at the water's edge.

He stripped to his shorts and socks, stuffed his shirt and jacket into one trouser leg to use as a pillow, then wiggled into his sleeping bag. A relic of his days in Vietnam, it was limp and patched with duct tape. Cappy twisted his neck until his head was comfortable against the makeshift pillow, then stared into the stars burning against the black sky.

He remembered nights when he and Darlene had taken a blanket to the beach and made love, then lain there, not speaking, not even touching, just looking into the depths of the universe. He never asked her what she was thinking of then, whether she was contemplating God and time, thinking of him or another man. Now Darlene probably could not even see the stars; her eyes had the flat sheen of the trout Jubal had pulled from the water, snatched from the only thing they knew by the lure of false fortune. What would she do with ten acres of land, facing away from all that was familiar, a razor in her brain and time dwindling?

Cappy wished he were a religious man, able to give himself to something higher and knowing. But he had never found that faith. In Vietnam, he had not prayed when the shooting started, just kept his head low and went by the manual. That seemed to be the only way that made any sense. You did not try to reason why the fellow next to you took a bullet and you didn't. Easier to keep your sanity that way. You didn't blame a God, or thank him either.

A meteor slipped across the heavens, breaking into three pieces before burning out. Its luminous trail lingered, and Cappy smelled the smoke again.

THE ANTI-AIRCRAFT BARRAGE began while the plane was still several minutes from the drop zone, the DC-3 bucking and shuddering through a hail of spent shrapnel. A shell burst close to the fuselage and riddled the underbelly with hot metal. The hot fragments tore holes in the floor, then passed through the ceiling. Sunlight shone eerily through the holes.

Buck Sergeant Clinton Tucker stared at dust floating in the shafts of light. He clicked the safety of his M-14 on and off methodically, his teeth grinding in anticipation of the next burst. He and nineteen other soldiers, laden with full combat gear, were on their maiden combat jump. Each of them stared into his own private vision, was alone with his thoughts.

"Stand up and hook in," the jump master told them. "We're thirty seconds from the drop zone." The drop zone was a small field on the outskirts of a Korean village. The place was surrounded by thick forest, where enemy troops were dug in.

Clinton tasted bile as he hooked into the static line. He had to look now where he had avoided looking the entire flight—the yawning hatch, bright with sunlight, black smoke streaming against the blue sky, the green and brown expanse of earth below. He was squad leader, first in line, with no man's back to guide him, no envelope of darkness. He tried to swallow the bile, took deep breaths.

"Move to the door," the jump master barked. "Go on my command."

Clinton felt the wind on his face and smelled the acrid smoke. Someone pressed a hand to his back, and he wondered whether the man behind him had his eyes closed. Clinton gripped the top of the hatch. He tried to close his eyes but could not.

"Go!"

The jump master tapped Clinton's shoulder. Below the plane he could see the small field, the roofs of the village. His hands tightened on the rungs above the door.

"Go, damn it!" the jump master roared. He struck Clinton on

the back. The man behind pushed against him. "Throw his ass out!" the jump master bellowed.

A quilt of whiteness surrounded Clinton; he no longer saw the ground or heard the jump master. He raised his feet against the rim of the hatch and shoved backward. The soldier behind him toppled, carrying down the man to his rear, tangling static lines and equipment. Clinton grabbed the legs of one of the men.

"God damn it!" the jump master roared. "Your ass is going to court-martial, soldier!"

When the plane had flown past the jump zone and was over enemy-infested forest, a shell hit its underbelly. The pilot banked the now burning plane sharply and turned back toward the village, but he was losing altitude fast.

"We're going in," the co-pilot shouted from the cockpit. "Get in crash positions."

Reality returned to Clinton as quickly as it had left him. He stood and stared into the purple face of the jump master, tried to speak but could not. The jump master slammed him against the bulkhead. "Put your harness on, soldier," he ordered. "I hope you survive this crash, so I can see you go to the brig."

Clinton slid down the bulkhead to a sitting position. The engines screamed as the pilot tried to stay level. The plane barely cleared the forest, crash-landing in the field where the men were to have jumped. The only one to survive was Clinton.

In the hospital he was awarded a Purple Heart, and after recovering from his wounds, he requested transfer to a ground unit. Despite the Silver Star and the two Bronzes he was awarded later for valor during combat, he kept his feet close to the ground—and his shame untold.

★ ★ ★

CAPPY WATCHED the glow of the meteor trail fade to blackness. Was it a good omen or a bad one, this chunk of light flung to earth? If only Darlene could have seen it. Her own light was receding, like the vapor trail. Would the end come for her as suddenly as a streak of light, or would she linger—and which was better?

She wants to be made honest, Cappy thought. She could have picked a better man. My life has been nothing but one long, wretched lie.

THE SIGN over the driveway read "Harmony Farm"; flowers and birds and rainbows were painted in pastel colors around the borders. Two large split geodes adorned either side of the road.

"Ain't them some pretty rocks," Glory said.

"Those are geodes." Kitty shifted into first and started forward. "They're igneous rocks, formed by volcanoes."

"I don't know about no igneous, but they pretty. I like to have me one."

The long paved driveway led across a lush pasture toward a large house at the foot of a mountain. Hand-painted signs were posted beside the driveway, announcing intermittently: "Love," "Friendship," "Peace," "Charity," "Forgiveness," "Tranquility." Glory read the words aloud as they passed.

"Looks like no fistfights here," she said. "Cappy, you gonna be bored to death."

"Probably a bunch of damn hippies," Cappy grumbled. "Wearing flowers and shit over their ears."

"They a lot of difference between flowers and shit," Glory said.

"Not to hippies."

As the bus reached the two-story Spanish-style house, the elaborate decoration became clear. The stucco walls were covered with bright murals: people of all colors standing naked among lions and tigers and snakes, butterflies and birds; a rainbow with a smiling sun shining above it; a big-gut Buddha sitting with his legs folded; angels playing trumpets and harps. Above the entrance was painted a huge, six-pointed star that radiated golden bolts of lightning.

"My gosh," Kitty said. "It looks like a cross between Raphael and Rousseau."

"Kitty, sometimes you talk like a college graduate," Glory said.

"I read a lot of books."

"Looks more like a cross between a six-year-old and a dopehead," Cappy said.

Kitty braked the bus to a stop beside a Volvo whose rear end was plastered with bumper stickers. One read: "Live Simply So Others Can Simply Live." Juniper and aspen trees were scattered across the front yard, their trunks painted like candy canes. In front of the house was a network of fish ponds; in a fountain, concrete bullfrogs spit water. A white peacock stared at the bus, tail plumes spread.

"I think we in the land of Oz," Glory said.

"Yeah," Jubal agreed, "and here comes two of the Munchkins."

From around the side of the house, a man and a woman walked hand in hand. Both wore loose white robes, and their heads were shaven. On top of the man's head was the image of a dove.

"We might be in heaven," Glory said. "Kitty, you didn't drive the bus off a cliff coming over here, did you?"

While Darlene stared through the window, everyone else

climbed out of the bus and waited as the couple approached. The woman lifted her hand in greeting.

"Welcome, and peace to you. Any friends of Jasper's are friends of mine."

"We're The Last Great Snake Show," Cappy said. "We haven't seen Jasper in a while."

"Isn't Jasper so sweet. I just love him to death." The woman extended her hand. "I'm Calico Dove, and this is my soulmate, Marvin."

Marvin offered a limp-fish handshake to Cappy, who then introduced himself, Glory, Jubal, and Kitty.

"Isn't that wonderful, Marvin." Calico pointed at the bus. "Jubilee Express. Such a peaceful message."

"How do you know Jasper?" Cappy asked. "I wouldn't put you guys together."

"Oh, Jasper is such a sweetheart. He just likes to act tough. I was actually married to him once, but I had to leave the Hollywood scene. I'm at peace now. I have Marvin and the colony."

"The colony?"

"I maintain an artists' colony here." Calico swept her hand in an arc. I own a thousand acres. There are currently fifty-three enlightened ones living in modest homes they designed themselves. We practice nonviolence, the universality of humankind. We're a happy mixture of what is good in the world."

Cappy nodded. "Y'all smoke a lot of dope, I reckon."

Calico laughed. "We use certain natural substances to enhance our third eye. We're primarily vegetarians, although we do eat certain types of flesh if it is cleanly raised. From what Jasper told me, I think all of you will fit in nicely. Jasper said you present a most delightful program."

"He didn't tell you what we do?" Glory asked.

"He only said you were into creative expression. He said you present a mind-opening program."

"Jasper said that?"

Marvin had not uttered a word. Cappy's eyes went to the dove on his head. "I like your bird. I go dove hunting every year. What kinda art you into?"

Marvin lifted his right index finger toward the sky.

"Marvin is observing a verbal fast," Calico said. "He is waiting for the Divine Consciousness to reveal to him the one true word. He has not spoken now for eight months."

Cappy patted Marvin on the shoulder. "Hang in there, bud. It'll come to you. Let me know when you find out."

"You seem to be such wonderful people," Calico said. "And to have evolved so from out of a culture that is bred of violence and bigotry. If the South can heal herself, there is hope for every nation and culture on earth."

"You been in the South much?" Cappy asked.

"Oh, never. I could not visit the American South any more than I could visit South Africa. But I channel energy there every afternoon at three twenty-one. I believe that is why you have come to us. Peaceful prophets from the evil side."

Cappy squinted at Glory. She winked. Marvin again lifted his finger toward the sky. Calico took Cappy's hand. "You can park your bus down at the creek, beside the cottonwoods. It is cool there, and the spirits speak from the tree boughs. You are most warmly invited to our humble communal meal at noon. We will seek your truths when the sun retires."

"Why that woman talk that way?" Glory asked when everyone was back on the bus. "She must think mighty slow."

"Aw, hell," Cappy said as he popped a beer. "Those two have probably watched *Easy Rider* five hundred times. Enlightened, my ass. Stoned out of their gourds is what they are."

They set up camp under a canopy of cottonwood trees alongside the creek. Assembling the stage and curtain had become easier now; it took Cappy and Jubal only about an hour. As the last nail was being pounded into place, a bell clanged from the big house and people began walking toward it.

"I hope we eat something better than Spam," Cappy said. He held Darlene's arm as everyone from the bus walked to the house.

A long table made of sheets of plywood on sawhorses sat in the shade of trees near the house. The seats ranged from blocks of wood to chaise longues. The table was set with an assortment of wooden and earthenware bowls, cups, and pitchers, and serving dishes full of food.

Several of the people were naked, a few wore only loincloths. Some had on white gowns like Calico and Marvin, others jeans and T-shirts, and one older man wore a tuxedo and polished shoes. All were Caucasian, with good teeth and clear skin and hands free of scars or calluses. Some of the men held hands, some of the women held hands, some men and women held hands. Some people were alone. All of them were somber.

"Don't drop your biscuit," Cappy whispered to Jubal. "I wouldn't chance bending over."

Calico and Marvin stood on one side of the table, greeting the enlightened ones by names that ranged from Fred to Moon Glow.

"We're so glad you came," Calico told Cappy as he approached. "We're happy to share our meager fare."

"I don't recognize much of this stuff," Cappy said. "Mind telling me what the blue-plate special is?"

Calico laughed. She pointed at the various dishes and described the contents. The meal included only the finest, freshest foods; free-range chicken breasts, soybean burgers, hummus, tofu, organically grown corn and potatoes, hydroponic greens and sprouts, whole wheat bread, extra-virgin olive oil, organic fruit. There were fresh juices, wine, a small keg of beer from a local microbrewery, and un-pasteurized milk.

"You guys don't skimp on the groceries, do you?" Cappy said.

"Lord, looks like homecoming," Glory said.

"The physical body is the vessel of the spirit," Calico said. "The healthier the physical body, the more enlightened the soul."

Calico scattered the members of the show among the colony residents at the table. Jubal had taken a bite of food when he saw that nobody else was eating; he laid down his fork. He sat between the man in the tuxedo and a young woman with a blue Mohawk and pierced ears, nose, and lip. Cappy sat between two naked men. He looked straight ahead, his hands in his lap.

When everyone was seated, Calico rose and rang a small bell. Everyone at the table stood, Cappy the last to do so.

"Peace and love to you and yours," Calico said. The residents repeated the words.

"We are delighted to have guests today to share our food. Tonight they will share with us their message." Calico named each member of the show, and in turn each nodded or smiled or, in Cappy's case, stared straight ahead. Calico grasped hands with Marvin, to her left, and a woman on her right. This was a signal for everyone around the table to do likewise. Cappy winced as the two naked men took his hands.

"We will now offer our thanks to the energies of goodness and peace. Clinton, would you like to lead us today?"

Cappy's head jerked toward Calico. The man to his left was smiling at him. "What?"

"Would you like as our guest to lead us in thanksgiving?"

"You mean the blessing?"

"Whatever you may call it."

Cappy turned his head skyward. In a life spent dining mostly in mess halls or juke joints, he was at a loss for words. Finally something came to him from boyhood: "Bless the meat and damn the skin, open your mouth and cram it in. Thank you, Lordy."

"YOU GONNA GET STRUCK DEAD, saying something like that." Glory fussed at Cappy after the meal was over and they were walking back to camp. "You don't fool around with the blessing."

"I don't know any blessings."

"I'll teach you some. 'Sides, I like the skin. Especially on fried chicken."

"You ever see such a meal?" Jubal asked. "Man, that was a spread."

"All that talk about simple food," Cappy said. "I was expecting rice and beans and water. Hell, I'm about half drunk."

"You're always about half drunk."

After an hour of what she called "digestive rest and reflection," Calico came to the camp. Jubal was fishing the creek; everyone else was trying to nap off the meal.

"Between two and four, we express our day's vision. Would you like to go and see some of the artists at work?"

"I would." Kitty stood up.

"I'll go too," Glory said.

"Just feel free to wander," Calico said. "Make yourselves at home."

Jubal came from the creek without any fish.

"You lost your touch?" Cappy asked him.

Jubal shook his head. "There's no fish in that water. I followed it upstream. It's manmade. The water comes out of a pump."

Cappy got up from his mattress after Glory had berated him for being antisocial. He made sure that Darlene was comfortable, then set out with the others to tour the colony. They first approached a small domed dwelling with skylights and solar panels. Inside, a young woman was painting at an easel. She was barefoot, wearing a loose, long dress and flowers in her hair.

"Hello," she said, and smiled. She had nearly finished the painting: a valley filled with stick-figure people and animals with bubble heads, all of them smiling. The sun smiled too, as did the moon, and the trees resembled giant flowers. On the edge of the easel was a marijuana cigarette.

"That's some happy place you got there," Glory said. "Must be heaven."

"We are in heaven now," the young woman said.

"Now?"

"We create heaven or hell by choice. I paint happiness, and live happiness in a world where evil cannot exist."

"What do those creatures eat?" Glory asked, pointing to the canvas.

"They need no food. Happiness fills their stomachs."

You were sure filling your stomach at lunch, Glory thought. There was a lot more on that table than happiness.

"This place of yours is pretty interesting," Cappy said. "Did you design it?"

"No. My daddy did."

"Did you build it?"

"No. My daddy had it built."

The young woman laid down her brush. Jubal studied the painting.

"That's a nice picture," he said. "You mind if I add something to it?"

"Go ahead."

In the middle of the canvas, Jubal painted a crude vulture with black paint, and surrounded it with a cage. He put the brush down.

"Why did you paint that?"

"Oh, I just needed a reason for all those animals and people to be so happy. Evil exists. We just have to try to cage it."

The woman removed the canvas from the easel and put a blank one on it. "I never thought of it that way. Where did you learn to paint?"

"I didn't. I just learned how to live."

"Will you paint me a picture?" the woman asked.

Jubal stared at Cappy. "Y'all go ahead. I'll catch up in a minute." He looked at the woman. "First you need to put that joint out," he told her. "It stinks."

The next dwelling was a tepee erected on top of a wooden deck. A window-unit air conditioner had been fitted into a hole in the side. A man and a woman who looked to be in their thirties were sitting at a card table, each bent over a laptop computer, pecking at the keys.

"Greetings," the man said. The woman continued typing.

"What are you writing?" Kitty asked.

"An alternative form of the novel that is minus conflict," the man said.

"How can you do that?"

The man pressed his curled fist against his forehead. "I understand you are from the South?"

"Yes. Where are you from?"

"From nowhere and everywhere. Southern literature—mind you, I am using quotation marks when I say 'literature'—is strewn with violence, prejudice, sexism, cruelty to animals. From Faulkner to Larry Brown, it is all the same. I assume the books are representative of the mindset of the people of such a crass culture. Unfortunately, those writings have leaked into the mainstream stores and libraries of America.

"Faulkner won the Nobel Prize," Kitty said.

"I do not recognize the Nobel Prize. It is an award for violence."

"How can you deny conflict? Creativity can be sparked by chaos and war and famine. Van Gogh cut off his own ear."

"Wait until my book is published," the man said. "Then you'll understand."

"Who's the publisher?" Kitty asked.

"I'm my own publisher. I will not sell out to the capitalistic New York publishing houses."

Cappy was more interested in the tepee. "I like your tent. But doesn't it get a little cold in the winter?"

"We don't winter here. We migrate like the birds to a colony in the Florida Keys."

"You must sell a lot of those self-published books," Kitty said.

"No. My father was a stockbroker and investor. Unfortunately, his greed induced a fatal heart attack when he was fifty-two. I'm now blessed to pursue a life devoted to revolutionizing the arts." The man looked down at his keyboard, then back at his visitors. "Just for the sake of argument, why is there so much violence in southern literature?"

"Think about it," Kitty said. "Where do the hurricanes hit land? Where was the Civil War fought? Where did slavery last, and blatant racism linger?"

"And you think that is good?"

"Not necessarily good, but it makes people want to tell their story. Isn't that what art is? People trying to make sense out of chaos."

The woman stopped typing and looked at Kitty. "That's not what Calico and Marvin are teaching us."

"What are they teaching you?" Kitty asked.

"That conformity is the path to enlightenment. That we all are a part of the great cosmic novel. That we must surrender to learn."

Kitty's face grew serious. "I could write a novel about conformity and surrender. Believe me, it would not end in enlightenment."

They went on to visit potters and sculptors, other writers and painters. One woman dabbed imaginary oils on a blank canvas, leaving viewers to picture whatever they desired. A man performed a song using only one word and one chord, repeated over and over. Cappy decided he and his companions wouldn't stop to chat with two naked men doing something with wet clay. So the group went on to an elaborate treehouse built in an oak, beneath which a woman danced stiffly to recorded flute music. Glory watched her awkward movements. "You need to get your hips into it, honey." She rotated her lower body.

The woman stopped, then wagged her hips from side to side.

"Like this." Glory put her hands on the woman's waist, then guided her rotation.

The woman giggled. "That feels good." She kept moving after Glory had removed her hands.

"Just let it go. Get your groove down. You got to loosen up the backbone."

The woman suddenly stopped dancing. "Carnal expression blocks the body's harmonic rivers."

"Say what?" Glory asked.

"Calico says my migraines come from sexual poisons. Tai chi releases the stress."

"I don't know about any tai chi," Glory answered. "I do know about headaches, though. The right man comes along, you won't use that tired ol' excuse."

DARLENE HAD BEEN LYING quietly in her bed; now she decided she had been stationary long enough. If you lie around waiting to die, you will, she told herself. She walked out of the bus, and felt the warm sun on her face, the sweet breeze, vigor stirring in her legs. She scanned the surrounding acres for people, but saw no one. The big house was only a few hundred yards away. Might as well be neighborly, she thought. They may be strange, but they seemed friendly enough. Slowly, she started on the gravel road.

At the front door, Darlene caught her breath and knocked. While she waited she noticed a sign above the door: "Enter in Peace."

I feel like I'm in pieces, she said to herself, but I guess I'm in peace too.

Darlene knocked again, but still there was no answer. She tried the door and found it unlocked, so she gingerly pushed it open. "Hello?" she said. Silence. When she stepped inside, she heard voices from a lighted room down a long hallway. She walked toward the light. Through the curtain of glass beads she could make out two figures—the couple who had greeted the bus earlier.

Marvin sat in front of a large glass-topped desk. The green glow of a computer cast a halo around his shaven head. He stared intently at the screen, and drew just as intently on a cigarette. A portable phone beside the computer buzzed; he reached for it without looking away from the screen.

"Hello. . . . Yeah, this is Marv." He sat up straighter in his chair. "Yeah, Harry. Thanks for returning my call. Look, I want to move immediately on that land bordering the ranch."

Marvin drew again on his cigarette, his forehead wrinkling while he listened to the man at the other end. "Fuck the Sierra Club," he blurted. "Fuck the Nature Conservancy, and the watershed too. I've got a list of people waiting for lots. We buy now, the grandfather clause will protect us."

He nodded or shook his head while uttering yes or no. "Do it!" he said finally, and clicked off the phone. He pushed back in his swivel chair and extended his legs.

Calico walked across the room and leaned against the desk to face him. "What did Harry say?"

"Ahhh! Fucking nature freaks are trying to get a court injunction to stop development of the southern slope. I'm a step ahead of them, though."

Calico touched the dove on Marvin's forehead with her index finger. Flakes of white fell. "You need to redo your tattoo. People might think it's fake."

"It *is* fake." Marvin smiled. "Maybe I'll put a turtle or a butterfly up there. I'll tell the deadheads that I went through a metamorphosis."

"Speaking of deadheads, what do you think of that bunch that rolled in on the bus?"

"Four rednecks and a nigger. What else are they? Why in hell did you let them come here?"

"The contracts do call for weekly spiritual enlightenment. Chanting monks get a little boring. Besides, Jasper says they're good. It'll remind us of the old days. And we owe Jasper some favors."

Marvin grunted his assent. "How are the meds, anyway? Do we need to get in touch with Jasper's connection?"

"Probably next week. The artists go through weed like a herd of cattle. The mushrooms are getting low too."

"Artists!" Marvin laughed. The phone buzzed again. He winked at Calico, then reached for the receiver.

Darlene backed away from the curtain and, as quietly and swiftly as she could, left the house.

LATER IN THE AFTERNOON, several dozen of the residents had gathered in a meadow. Glory was instructing women in dance, while a group of men and women sat around Jubal. He held a corn snake and a king snake in his hands. Cappy was before another group, gesturing emphatically. He looked up to see Marvin and Calico approaching. Neither was smiling.

"What are you doing?" Calico asked one of the men listening to Cappy.

"Debating war."

"There would be no war if it was never debated," Calico said.

"Bullshit," Cappy answered. "Ignoring something unpleasant doesn't make it go away. It just gets worse."

At the sound of Calico's voice, silence descended over her colony of artists. When Marvin raised his arm and pointed, they immediately returned to their homes.

THE FLAMES of twilight spiked skyward above the mountain, and the air was cooling rapidly, as the audience assembled for The Last Great Snake Show. All the people were dressed now, in crimson robes that trailed to their ankles, with hoods over their heads; they all wore shoes, and each of them carried his own single-leg wooden stool. They congregated in front of the stage, some waving to the members of the show and shouting greetings. They seated themselves by squatting on the stools with feet wide apart, backs straight, heads erect.

"It's kinda spooky," Jubal said. "Everyone looks alike."

Cappy surveyed the crowd. "They goddamn don't know carpentry. Who ever heard of a one-legged stool."

"It looks like something used in yoga," Kitty said. "To stimulate balance and attention."

"I doubt they use it when they're drinking. At least they got clothes on tonight. Glad I dressed." Cappy was in his Confederate uniform.

Darlene sat at the rear of the stage on one of Harmony Farm's chaises, a blanket over her legs. She had not yet told Cappy what she had heard in the house. Let him do the show first and get paid, she thought.

Calico and Marvin walked to the front of the assembled crowd. Marvin sported a new false tattoo, a turtle, on his white scalp. Calico, still and erect as she stared above the heads of the people, held aloft a quartz crystal.

"Ode to the day," she said.

"And the day was good," the multitude responded in unison.

"Repentance for yesterday," Calico continued.

"For the sins of our fathers."

"Faith in tomorrow."

"For we are the enlightened."

Slowly she lowered the crystal. "We are gifted tonight with visitors from a land so unlike the small planet we have pioneered. A land of hostility and greed, of prejudice and bigotry and violence. But they are of the enlightened ones, sent to us to share their message of hope and change."

Matches flared as people in the congregation lit cigarettes. The smoke was blue in the dim lights from the stage, the marijuana smell heavy.

Behind the curtain, Cappy smoothed wrinkles on his uniform. Jubal prepared the rattler. Glory studied herself in a hand mirror. She was dressed as Eve, with willow branches woven together and duct-taped to her G-string. Sycamore leaves covered her nipples. Beside the tape player, Kitty nervously jiggled her foot up and down.

Cappy swallowed the last of a beer, threw the can off the back of the stage, and stepped through the curtain. He squinted in the bright lights.

"Ladies and gentlemen," he began, "I welcome you tonight—"

"Please don't address us in such sexist terms," Calico's voice rang out.

"What?"

Calico smiled. "You are a visitor and not familiar with our customs. We do not differentiate our worthiness according to gender. We are creatures of the light."

Cappy chewed his bottom lip, then nodded. "Creatures of the light," he said, "direct to you from the land of Dixie—"

"That word is not of our vocabulary," Calico announced.

"What word?"

"D-I-X-I-E. We have removed ourselves from regionalism. We are of one people."

Cappy shook his head. "All right. Direct to you from North Carolina. Gloria Peacock, black as a brier berry and just as sweet, raised on the old Negro hymns. She brings to you tonight a variation on what really happened in the Garden of Eden."

"'Negro' is not in our vocabulary." Calico was still smiling sweetly. "If you must differentiate between races, please use the term 'African-American.'"

Cappy's jaw dropped. "Just open the goddamn curtain," he shouted.

"We do not use the word 'God.' We are all equal in our worthiness."

Kitty pushed a button on the tape player, and "Swing Low, Sweet Chariot" resounded from it. She pulled the rope to part the curtain, revealing Jubal holding handfuls of snakes. Glory lay on the stage as if asleep, then stirred as if awakening, then sprang to her feet in an energized dance.

"Do it, Gloria!" came shouts from the audience. "Swish it, honey!"

From the stage Glory could see Calico turn to Marvin. He narrowed one eye.

Glory took a large king snake from Jubal and wrapped it around her neck. She leaped from the stage to the ground in front of the audience. With one hand she raked the leaves from her breasts and, winking at a man who smiled at her from beneath his hood, squeezed one nipple. He toppled from his stool and unseated the people around him; a dozen people found themselves on the ground. Glory meanwhile spun and shook her buttocks, and continued to grin at the crowd. She pranced back onstage, as the topplers in the audience got up.

Jubal took the king snake from Glory, then dropped all the snakes from his hands into a bucket and closed the lid. A hooded figure stood up in the middle of the audience, then pushed the hood back to reveal herself as the young artist whom Jubal's group had met earlier.

She shouted Jubal's name.

He peered into the crowd. "Oh, hey," he said when he recognized her. "What's up?"

The woman unrolled a canvas and held it above her head. On it was the lifelike image of a king snake, coiled in a death grip around a rattler. "I painted this for you," she told Jubal. "It'll protect you."

He lifted his thumb in the air. He noticed Calico nudge Marvin with her elbow, then whisper to him.

Jubal handed a rubber snake to Glory, then opened another bucket and dumped the contents—a rattlesnake—on the floor. He knelt and captured the serpent behind the head before it had time to coil and begin rattling. Glory gyrated around him, flogging herself with the rubber snake.

Several other people in the audience removed their hoods. Others stood to see better. A few were moving their hips in rhythm with the music.

"Stop it!" a voice roared above the music, Pink Floyd now. "Stop it this instant!" Marvin had walked to the front of the audience. His face was pale. "This is not art. It is violence and sexism. I will not let my people witness this spectacle of degradation."

Cappy motioned for Kitty to stop the music. "You finally found your voice, didn't you, buddy?" Cappy said. "What's the one true word?"

Calico stood beside Marvin. "Is this a parody? Should we look deeper for the message you wish to share with us?"

"This is The Last Great Snake Show," Cappy said. "What you see is what you get. It's called entertainment."

Calico walked to the edge of the stage. "I should have known not to trust Jasper ever again. I should have known even better that anything from the South could not be enlightenment. You wear a military uniform in this refuge of peace. You present a poor African-American woman who has not left the bondage of her forefathers. You dominate and subject animals to cruelty, as though humankind were superior."

"That was a rubber snake, lady," Jubal said.

Marvin raised one fist above his head and slowly scanned the audience. "People, can't you understand what is happening here? Expression and art cannot come at the expense of one another." He walked into the crowd, where the young woman still held the snake picture overhead. He took it from her, ripped the canvas down the middle, then turned to address Cappy. "If we were not a people of peace, I would personally lead the movement to remove you from our refuge."

"We'll go, bud," Cappy answered. "Give us what we're owed, and we'll be out of here in an hour."

"I will not aid the enemy," Calico said. "You came here in deception, and now you ask me to give you money."

"We agreed on a price. We brought a show. I want my money."

"Money is not the answer to the world's problems."

"That's easy for you to say. You seem to have all you need."

"I believe in redemption, in the power of reform. I'll make you a deal."

"Name it."

"Denounce the uniform you are wearing. Confess your racism and bigotry and ignorance, and I will give you your money." Calico reached into an opening in her robe. She removed a thick roll of bills.

"Confess your sins," Marvin said. "I know the one true word, and I will share it with you. Purity is yours through confession."

"The one true word is 'hypocrisy'!" The blanket dropped to Darlene's feet as she stood at the back of the stage. "I wouldn't take your money if I was starving," she said, coming forward. "You're all a bunch of pampered rich kids who can afford to eat your pricey organic food while denouncing everything this country has given you. You call yourselves enlightened, but you're so blinded by your hypocritical bigotry that you pretend you're free. You play your word games, pretend you're artists and freethinkers. I wouldn't want to live in your world."

She pointed toward Marvin. "You better open your eyes, kiddies. Go rub a little water on the great one's new tattoo and see how quickly it dissolves. You're not total zombies yet."

Now Glory joined in. "While we're getting personal," she shouted, "don't none of you go calling me *African*-American. I wouldn't go back to no stinking jungle, even if they made me queen. I'm nigger to the bone, and proud of it. Ain't nobody *making* me dance up here. Talk about slaves, what about all you sitting there on them ridiculous stools, looking like the Klan in them robes?"

Glory singled out a woman who had been dancing near the stage. "Take that robe off, honey, and come on with us. I could use some backup. You the one in chains."

"Go back to your dwellings," Marvin ordered. "Go now!"

The woman who had danced held Glory's eyes momentarily, then pulled her hood back over her head. She joined the rest of the audience, who steadily filed away from the stage and left the meadow. On Cappy's command, Kitty pulled the rope to draw the curtain closed.

I GUESS THAT just about does it." Cappy lowered his fifth beer of the hour. "That about takes the cake."

They were a hundred miles from Harmony Farm, having packed up in the dark. Jubal was at the wheel, Kitty writing a postcard, the others staring into the darkness beyond the windows.

"Getting sloshed ain't going to help," Glory said.

"It ain't going to hurt." Cappy turned the can up again. "They wouldn't even fight us. At least old Reginald was willing to fight for what he wanted. I'd love to have knocked that turtle off Marvin's head."

"They'd have fought if you had tried to take their dope and fancy little houses," Darlene said. "All that enlightenment bullshit. They'd have fought hard if it was up to them."

"Yeah, I seen their kind before. Got hit by an egg from one when I came home from 'Nam. White middle-class punks living good and free because of the sacrifices their parents and grandparents made for them."

"So what's the game plan now?" Jubal asked. "Which way you want this bus pointed?"

Cappy pulled his wallet from his jeans and took out the piece of paper with the information from Jasper. He looked at the last entry. "Freedom Ranch," he read aloud. "Whitewater, Idaho. We probably shouldn't even go there, but it's on the list."

"When are we supposed to be there?" Jubal asked.

"Not for another damn week."

"I like the name," Glory said. "Freedom. Maybe they won't be trying to tell folks what words to use."

Cappy snorted. "We don't know what their interpretation of freedom is."

"Looks like we're going to need to hit a couple more small towns on the way," Jubal told him.

"You saw what happened last time."

"We'll go by the books. Get a permit. Only let in adults."

"What are we going to buy a permit with?" Cappy replied. "Our good looks?"

KITTY LISTENED on and off to the conversation. She tried to concentrate on the postcard:

Dear Esther,

Please don't worry about me. I believe I'm in the safest hands I could be in. In the past two weeks I've really come to know the people I'm with like family, and finally—maybe—I'm starting to know myself. When we're together again, I'll tell you some stories that you will find hard to believe. I better close now and get some sleep.

Love always,
Cornelia

In the morning, after a night at another rest stop, Kitty steered the bus into Wheat, Colorado. The town smelled like a stockyard and seemed to be populated only by cowboys. Kitty pulled into a small parking lot off the main street.

"I'll be surprised if they let us set up a show," Cappy said.

"This is the real West," Glory reassured him. "They fond of titties and snakes out here."

"They're fond of lynching people too." Cappy stood, looking through the bus door toward the courthouse.

"Let me go," Kitty told him. "Let me talk to them."

"What makes you think you can get a permit and I can't?"

"Let her go," Darlene said. "It makes sense."

"What sense?"

"She's young and innocent-looking."

"She's a kid!"

Darlene glared at Cappy. "Let her go, Cap."

He slammed his fist into his other palm. "All right, dammit. I guess I ain't considered worth a shit no more." He nodded toward Kitty. "Go ahead. Get us a permit to do a titty-and-snake show." He handed her his last two twenty-dollar bills. "While you're at it, get a free one. Hell, see if they'll lock me up for about a year. I'd probably be better off."

"Don't get in such a tizzy again," Glory told him. "One of these days, you gonna give yourself a stroke!"

A THIN WOMAN in a flannel shirt, her face brown and leathery, sat at a desk inside the courthouse.

"How are you, ma'am?" Kitty asked.

"'Ma'am'? I don't hear that word much. I'm fine. How are you?"

"Very well, thank you." Kitty clasped her hands tightly at her waist. "I need to ask a question."

"Then ask it."

"Where does someone go to get a permit in this town?"

"Permit for what?"

"I'm—I'm not quite sure how to categorize what I need. My friends and I—we're parked outside—we have a traveling show. We would like to do a performance tonight."

"Performance?" The woman searched Kitty's face, then walked to the window. "Jubilee Express. Are you a gospel group?"

"We do have a lot of spirit in the program."

"I don't know that we issue permits for traveling gospel groups. But you can speak to the district judge. He happens to be here to-day."

The woman walked to her desk and spoke into a phone, then directed Kitty through a door into a small office. An elderly man sat back in his chair, a Stetson hat on his desk.

"Howdy, Miss. How can I help you?"

Kitty closed the door and sat in the chair he offered her. "Your Honor, I was hoping to apply for an entertainment permit."

"You don't have to be formal. My name is Lewis. I understand you're a gospel group?"

Kitty clasped her hands again. She shifted forward in her chair. "Actually, to be truthful, we're not exactly that."

"What are you, then?"

"Do you have a county fair?"

"No. Just the big state fair."

"What about carnivals?"

"We have rodeos."

Kitty nodded. "We have a program that involves live animals and dancing."

"You mean monkeys and stuff."

"No. Snakes."

"What sort of dancing?"

Kitty fidgeted. She took a deep breath and looked the judge straight in the eyes. "I guess you might call it a striptease."

The judge swallowed hard, then sat forward himself.

"You don't look like a stripper, honey."

"Oh, it's not me. I just drive the bus and cook."

The judge rested his hands on his desk and nodded. "I served a stint with the Eighty-second Airborne down in North Carolina. There was a place called Rick's Lounge. The women didn't use snakes, though."

"We have a man who handles the snakes. He catches them bare-handed and milks them. It's a really good show."

"Where are you people from?"

"North Carolina."

The judge rocked back in his chair and laughed. "I should have known. Sweetheart, out here we shoot snakes."

"Could we get a permit, then?"

"It'll cost you."

"How much?"

"Oh . . ." He pursed his lips. "About a hundred dollars."

Kitty dug into her pocket. She peeled off a hundred from the bills she had left.

"About two hundred."

"You said a hundred!"

"I reconsidered."

Kitty placed two bills on the desk. The judge pocketed them, then took a sheet of paper, wrote down some words, and signed his name. He handed the paper to Kitty.

"You can set up in the park just west of town for two nights. I'll alert the sheriff. Any fighting breaks out, someone is liable to get arrested. Prostitution is illegal."

Kitty blushed. "We have nothing to do with that."

The judge leaned forward again. "Miss, you look like you ought to be in college or something."

"Believe me, sir, I am getting an education right here."

"I CAN'T UNDERSTAND IT." Cappy held the permit and the two twenties.

"You ought to apologize," Glory said. "Kitty done bailed us out again."

"She has a definite way with words," Darlene said.

Kitty ignored the praise and sat in the driver's seat. The engine struggled, then grumbled and backfired. As she stared through the dusty windshield, the smile she had been wearing flattened.

AT A USED CLOTHING STORE in the town, Kitty and Glory searched through the racks for a cowgirl outfit. The theme of the next show, Glory had decided, needed to fit the town. For less than ten dollars they walked out with a red skirt fringed with white, a matching blouse, a red cowgirl hat, and a pair of worn white boots.

"A little polish and a stitch here and there, I be looking like Annie Oakley," Glory said.

Kitty was silent as they walked to the park where Jubal and Cappy were setting up the stage. Occasionally, she stopped and taped a flyer to a post or wall.

DIRECT TO YOU

FROM THE HEART OF DIXIE

THE LAST GREAT SNAKE SHOW

A STAGE PRODUCTION OF SERPENTS AND SEXUALITY

TWO NIGHTS ONLY

(guns checked at the door)

"Why you so quiet, Miss Kitty?" Glory chuckled. "Miss Kitty! We ought to put you on the stage. Do a *Gunsmoke* show. Cappy, his ol' ill ass just born to be Doc.

"You look sad, Kitty. What's wrong?"

Kitty shrugged. "Nothing, really. I just feel like a tagalong. You and Jubal and Cappy are working so hard, and all I do is heat up beans and drive the bus."

"Honey, I have to admit I had my doubts about you at first. But you been redeeming yourself double-time. You found that money when we needed it so bad. You sprang Cappy out of jail. You got us this permit for free. You 'bout the luckiest person I ever met."

"But you and the others put your bodies up there. Jubal even endangers his life. I just shift gears and operate a can opener."

"You do more than that, honey. You like a good-luck charm. 'Sides, you don't have enough ass to shake it onstage. Men be throwing rocks."

When Kitty didn't smile, Glory reached and tousled her hair. "I'm just kidding, white girl. You part of the team."

FOR THE FIRST NIGHT, not even twenty people showed up. At ten dollars a head, the earnings were disappointing. But when the curtain closed, the audience cheered and clapped until Glory agreed to an encore. Cappy passed the hat and collected an additional thirty dollars.

"That was a hell of a show," one cowboy said, drunkenly slapping Cappy on the back. "I never seen such a thing. I'm coming tomorrow night with all my buddies."

"You are prime meat," a woman told Jubal. She handed him a ten-dollar bill. "Here's a down payment on tomorrow night. My girlfriends have to see this."

AFTERWARD, sitting by the camp light, Cappy counted bills. "Maybe our luck has turned. I'm holding cash for a change."

Jubal left the circle of light and walked to a makeshift bench, a board on cinder blocks, some yards away. Kitty watched him sit down and look at the sky. She hesitated several minutes before walking toward him.

"Mind if I join you?" she asked. "There's a lot of bugs around that lamp."

"Sure. If this board don't break. It's about rotten." He made room for her.

"What are you looking at?" Kitty asked.

"I don't know. Nothing, I guess. Mostly just thinking about back home."

"Are you homesick?"

"Kinda. I never been away before. I spent my whole life near the ocean. It sure is different out here."

"When do you think you'll go back?"

"That's hard to say. When we get Darlene to her land, we've still got to feed her. Got to have a place to stay. Maybe I can hire on a fishing boat."

"What do you think Miss Darlene's future is? I mean . . ."

"I know what you mean. Not long. She's a tough old bird, but she's getting weaker every day. She wants to see her land. She might just slip away then.

"What about you, Kitty? I guess you'll be getting off soon?"

"Getting off?"

"You said you were going to the Tetons. After we leave here, we'll be going right close to them."

Kitty hadn't been thinking about the Tetons in days. She knew her money was dwindling. But more than that, she was enjoying the company.

"I—I guess so."

Jubal nodded. "I best get some sleep. Big show tomorrow." When he pressed down on the plank to rise, it snapped in the middle, pitching him and Kitty toward each other. Jubal hit the ground first; Kitty sprawled across his chest. She shrieked at first, then laughed with him.

"You all right?" Jubal asked.

"I'm fine. I just mashed you nearly to death, that's all." Kitty lay on her side against Jubal's chest, her head close to his. She knew she should move, but even more strongly she knew she did not want to. She could feel his breath against her neck.

"I guess I should get up," she said.

"I guess so," Jubal replied, his voice thick.

Kitty pushed against his chest as she stood. She extended her arm and helped him to his feet. He squeezed her hand slightly before releasing it.

"Good night," he said.

Kitty watched his silhouette moving toward the light. She felt a knot in her stomach, a wonderful, shimmering ache she had never felt before.

MOST OF THE PEOPLE walking in the park gave more than a passing glance to the black woman sitting on the bench. They like to look, Glory figured. Think I'm an oddball. Guess I am, out here. If one of them would stop long enough to talk, I'd tell them a thing or two.

Close to where she sat was a statue of an Indian, heavily marked with pigeon droppings and graffiti. Looks like you ain't in no hurry, Tonto, Glory commented silently. Let me tell *you* a thing or two. . . .

I'm starting to believe all the black people in this country live in the South. They sure don't live in the West. Ain't seen hardly two black faces since we passed over the Mississippi. I get some looks too. We be at the gas station or McDonald's and people stare, like I'm something strange to them. That ol' woman back in that big ol' house had me sitting at a different table; I've heard "nigger" more than once on this trip. Talk about racism and prejudice in the South . . .

I ain't gonna defend the South; it plain and simple that there's white people there who never liked the likes of me and never will. There's probably a lot more black skeletons hid under the earth than the police will ever know about too. But there's some white skeletons also. I seen my mama spit many a time when talking about white people.

But I have to say this about home: We always had to try and get along, 'cause we were thrown in together.

I think back to the tobacco fields where I worked each summer till I left home—now, that was a time. Sticky leaves and the hot sun, gnats in the air and those big, ugly tobacco worms. Never was harder work. But there wasn't no color 'cept green. Green tobacco and green money. I be working right alongside white girls, for the same money, and the talk that would go on. They was mostly women at the barn. The men be in the fields. No difference between us—we'd all talk men and babies and who wore what to church. Between trailers of tobacco, we'd line up at the water cooler and everybody drink from the same tin cup. You hot and tired and that water cold, color ain't no matter. Come lunchtime, we all pile in the bed of a pickup and ride down to the store and eat pork and beans and saltine crackers and honey buns and drink Pepsi-Colas. That was some of the best times.

Course, we went our separate ways at church time, and at school there be separate groups. The basketball team was about half and half, and in my junior year, a black gal was named homecoming queen. Now, I don't mean to sugar-coat it. In my senior year, the school got closed down for three days 'cause of fighting between blacks and whites, and the police had to step in. Most of the trouble was between the white-trash rednecks and niggers walking around with a Afro pick stuck in their hair, looking like fools. They didn't want to be in school, nohow.

I guess what I'm saying is, you knew where you stood. This girl might call you a nigger, and this other girl you shared biology lab with. You knew who was a friend, and who was the enemy.

Out here, I feel like a loner. I bet right now I'm the only black woman in fifty square miles. And the people either stare at me or look away like I'm invisible.

BY SHOWTIME, the tent was packed with men and women. Kitty had bought a cassette at the thrift shop, and she put it on—"Oklahoma!" was the first song—to open the curtain. Glory was onstage in her cowgirl outfit, twin cap revolvers in holsters at her waist. By the end of the set, she wore only the gun belt, both pistols in her hands as she fired into the air. The crowd stood, cheering and clapping.

During his act, Jubal had to taunt the rattler more than usual to make it react. The snake had gotten used to him. Still, the audience gasped each time the snake struck toward his decoy hand, and the people roared when he captured the serpent and stood, holding it aloft.

He was about to leave the stage when a cowboy stepped forward holding a burlap bag.

"I bet you a hundred you can't catch this one inside a minute," the man said, loud enough for the audience to hear.

Jubal stared at him. "What you have in there?"

"The biggest damn western diamondback I ever saw."

At the back of the tent, Darlene shook her head.

"Inside a minute?"

"I have a stopwatch. I'll call out the seconds."

"A hundred dollars?"

"Got it right in my wallet."

Darlene shook her head again.

"Hand me the bag," Jubal said.

Kitty followed the transaction, nervously clutching the front of her shirt.

Cappy took a step forward. "We don't need the money," he told Jubal.

The bag was heavy, the snake already buzzing. Jubal walked to center stage, ignoring the rest of the crew. "Start the watch when I drop the bag on the floor," he instructed.

The bag hit the plywood with a thud, and immediately the snake emerged in a coil, its rattling tail a blur. The serpent was long, at least six feet, and massive. Its head was nearly as wide as Jubal's palm.

"One," the cowboy shouted.

Jubal crouched; the snake raised its head to the strike position. Immediately it lunged, and Jubal jerked back, with only a second to spare. The snake coiled again, its black tongue flickering in the air.

Jubal held out his decoy hand and moved his catch hand in. The snake struck again, before he was even close.

"Fifteen."

Kitty shrieked when the rattler struck a third time.

"Thirty."

"Let the damn snake go!" Cappy shouted.

Jubal stared into the snake's dark eyes: Bad-ass, ain't you. He moved his hand closer. You're not failing me again, hand. I'm holding on. I'm not going to fail again.

"Forty-five."

The audience was silent. Jubal could hear his pulse in his ears. He knew he was out of range, but at fifty-five seconds, he lashed out. He seized the snake's neck, lower than usual. The rattler twisted its head down and sank one fang into Jubal's thumb.

Jubal worked his catch hand higher to rip the fang from his flesh. He stood, wielding the beast over his head. The crowd was stunned; then everyone burst into a roar of clapping and foot-stomping.

"Keep the damn snake," the cowboy said. He threw a crumpled bill onto the stage.

Jubal's hands were trembling as he returned the rattler to the burlap sack. A spot of blood had beaded on his thumb. He nodded for Kitty to start the music for Glory's next number, and left the stage, the audience still thundering behind him.

Cappy met him at the bus. "That thing bite you?"

"Hell, yeah! Got me with one fang." He held his hand up.

"Jesus Christ. Where's a fucking hospital?"

"Cut me, Cap. We can't afford no hospital. Cut me."

Cappy locked eyes with Jubal.

The fang had entered at an angle, and the venom was deposited just under the skin. Already the bite was beginning to swell.

"You need to be in a hospital."

"Cut me. I know what I'm talking about. Andy cut me once when a cottonmouth tagged me. The venom hasn't had time to circulate. Cut me right here."

Cappy's chest heaved as he unfolded his pocketknife. "This is going to hurt."

"It'll hurt worse if you don't. Cut an X right over the puncture. Don't go too deep."

Jubal stiffened when Cappy sliced through his skin. After the knife was removed, Jubal squeezed his thumb, milking it upward from the base. Blood flowed freely, mixed with yellow streaks of venom. When he saw only red, he put his thumb in his mouth and sucked, trying to draw out any last drops of poison. Cappy then poured a cool stream of rubbing alcohol over the wound.

From inside the tent they could hear the hoots and catcalls of Glory's satisfied audience.

"We didn't need the money." Darlene scolded Jubal late that night as they ate supper around the camp lantern.

"It was a hundred bucks. You see this steak I'm eating? All it cost me was a cut hand."

"You need stitches," Kitty said.

"It'll heal."

"It could have cost you your life," Cappy said.

"We needed the money."

"Jubal, the money doesn't matter," Darlene said. "You know that. There's a whole lot more going on here than money."

Jubal said nothing, and cut into his steak.

"Well," Cappy said, "we made a little more than six hundred dollars tonight. Unless a tornado drops in here, we might just get to keep this money for a change."

"How long will it take us to get to the next gig?" Jubal asked.

"It's about a two-day ride. We'll swing toward Jackson and let Kitty off at the Tetons, and the next day we'll be at the last pervert on the list."

Kitty stared at her plate. "If it's all the same with everyone, I'd like to stay on with the show. Till we get to Miss Darlene's land." Kitty glanced at Jubal, then stared at her plate.

"Lord, Kitty, that would be wonderful," Glory said.

"You're welcome till we reach Timbuktu if you like," Cappy said.

Jubal's face lifted slowly in a smile.

THE LAST GREAT SNAKE SHOW rolled out of town with coolers full of food and the gas tank topped off and a little more than four hundred dollars in cash. Everyone was feeling confident for the first time in days, as if bad luck had been left behind. Those optimistic feelings didn't last much beyond the Idaho state line, however, where a harsh grinding noise began underneath the chassis. Jubal, who was driving, succeeded in bringing the limping bus to a service station in the next town. There, a mechanic confirmed what Cappy and Jubal feared most: The rebuilt transmission had gone out, and there was no repairing it.

"I got one that come out of a school bus that'll fit," the mechanic said.

"How much?" Cappy asked.

The man rolled his cigarette across his lips. "I rebuilt the whole thing. Including labor, it'll run about six hundred dollars."

"The whole bus ain't worth six hundred dollars." Cappy shuffled his feet, then looked up at the mechanic. "If it makes any difference, we're a gospel group."

"I'm sorry. That's the best I can do," the mechanic replied. "I have to make a living too."

"We'll get another permit," Jubal told Cappy. "We'll earn the money."

"Boy, our *luck* and our *time* is running out!"

The mechanic left Cappy and Jubal and went inside the service station. Kitty, who had been following the conversation, headed for the rest room. She pulled the remaining bills from her pocket and counted them, and pressed them against her forehead. She could see Cappy and Jubal still arguing beside the bus when she came out of the rest room.

"Psssst," she hissed at the mechanic.

He turned toward her.

"Can you come here for a second?"

The man walked over, frowning.

"Is that transmission price rock-bottom?"

"I can't go no lower."

"Can I make a deal with you?"

A grin spread over the man's face. "I thought you people were religious, sis."

"I don't mean that type of deal." Kitty held out her money. "Here's five hundred dollars. I want you to tell the older man that you have another transmission that you can sell him for a hundred. Put the one you told him about in, but don't let on that I paid you."

"Why the secrecy?"

"I owe them a favor." Kitty put the money into the man's hand, then returned to the bus.

"I don't want to set up again," Cappy was saying. "The law

might not be so lenient here." He saw the mechanic approaching from the garage.

"Hey, fellow," the man called.

"Yeah," Cappy said sourly.

"Look. You being church people, I'll cut you a break."

"What?"

"I have another transmission that'll fit. It's not rebuilt, but it's not broke either."

"How much?"

"For you, a hundred dollars, labor included."

Cappy's eyes widened. "Praise God. Will it get us to Oregon?"

"Money-back guarantee."

"Put it in, brother."

INSTALLING THE TRANSMISSION was an all-day task, so Kitty, Cappy, and Jubal took turns driving through the night to stay on schedule for Freedom Ranch. They crossed the Bitterroot Range, ears popping, the wind chilly through the windows, then dropped into the high desert of central Idaho. Dawn was about to drown the stars when Cappy wheeled into a truck stop on the outskirts of Cody. He shut down the engine and almost immediately fell asleep, his head supported by the steering wheel.

JUBAL WAS THE FIRST to awaken in the morning. He heard the songs of birds mixing with the rumble of diesel engines, and tried to patch together his memory: what had happened the day before, where they were now, where they were going.

Kitty lay on a mattress beside him, in the jeans and shirt she had worn the day before. She was on her back, her face turned toward his, her thin lips apart. She had such perfect teeth, he noticed, and such clear pale skin; a vein showed on one cheek. Her nose was thin and straight, and her chin unusually strong for a woman. She wasn't exactly beautiful, Jubal thought, but pretty in a strange way, with a mixture of fragility and strength. He found it hard to imagine she had grown up in an orphanage; she looked almost regal, spoke a fancy English, and had the manners of someone used to eating with real silver on linen tablecloths.

Jubal cared for her, and hated that he did. Loving someone always seemed to end in pain, and either blaming yourself or being blamed for what happened. That night when the plank had broken, he had liked her lying against him, had even wanted to put his arms around her and hold her. But he didn't know how she felt about him, and besides, she had said she was getting off at the Tetons. Now here she was, lying beside him, and the Tetons were behind them.

Kitty moved in her sleep, and her face was even closer to Jubal's, her forehead almost against his mouth. Very slowly and gently, he pressed his lips against her, tasting her skin with the tip of his tongue.

BLACK BLOCK LETTERS on a simple wooden sign above a gate announced the entrance to Freedom Ranch. A flag with three black X's on a bright red background rippled on a metal flagpole. The gate was unlocked, so Jubal pushed it open; he waited for Kitty to drive through, then closed it. The gravel road that led to the ranch house was dotted with cow manure; it ran between pastures of coarse brown grass, where cattle looked up chomping as the bus went by.

The ranch house sat on the side of a hill, a big two-story log prefab. Behind it were a barn, twin silos, and assorted machinery. As the bus approached, three Dobermans and a mastiff barked and ran beside the tires. A pickup truck was parked in front of the house. Kitty geared down and stopped the bus beside the truck. Outside, the dogs roared.

"I ain't going out there," Cappy said. "Toot the horn."

Kitty tapped the horn three times. The dogs barked even louder.

"I don't think they into love and peace too much," Glory said.

A minute passed, and the front door opened. A large man dressed in black walked out, a Colt .45 on his hip. He leaned on the porch banister and looked at the bus, then headed down the steps. He shouted at the dogs, which immediately stopped barking and retreated behind him.

As he approached, everyone on the bus could see just how big the man was, well over six feet, thick sculpted arms bursting out of a tight T-shirt. His head was bald, and he sported a bushy black mustache. Sewn onto the shoulders of the T-shirt were miniature flags like the one by the gate.

"Looks like Rambo," Cappy said. "You girls stay on the bus." He opened the door and stepped down, followed by Jubal. The dogs kept up a low growl but stayed where they were.

"Howdy, folks," the man said. "You must be the Captain." He extended his arm.

"I'm Clinton Tucker." Cappy grasped the man's hand. "This here is Jubal Lee."

"Ah, the snake man." He shook Jubal's hand. "I'm Virgil Barton, and this is my spread you see here. I've been looking forward to your visit. There's not much to do around here but work."

"We're here to entertain, that's for sure," Cappy said. "How do you know Jasper, if you don't mind me asking?"

"I used to be a stunt man. Did a few of his films. Even had a couple of speaking roles. But I gave up on the system a few years back and moved out here. I'm a lot happier now."

"You have a nice place."

"I'm with my own kind out here." Virgil looked through the bus door at Kitty and Glory. "Got some cuties in there. Jasper said you really get down-and-dirty. Snakes and sin. Me and the fellows are ready to loosen up a bit."

Cappy followed his gaze to Kitty. "Actually, that young girl's not the one that . . ."

"See that barn back there?" Virgil said. "That's where you can set up your stage. I got to go to town and get some folding chairs from the union hall. We're expecting about a hundred people."

Virgil shook hands again with Cappy and Jubal, glanced once more at Kitty, then walked to his truck. He called the dogs into the bed and drove away.

Jubal watched the truck recede. "Right nice fellow."

"Seems more normal than most of Jasper's crowd," Cappy replied. "I'm not too sure of those patches on his shoulders, though."

THE BARN was so big that Kitty was able to drive the bus inside. The concrete floor had been swept clean, tools and sacks of feed stacked against the walls. Swallows, which nested in the rafters, twittered and darted overhead.

"I don't like being inside with no birds." Glory crossed her heart. "That's a bad omen."

"It only applies to houses," Jubal said.

"Well, this as big as one."

WHILE JUBAL AND CAPPY busied themselves with the stage and Glory attended to Darlene, Kitty watched the men work. She had asked to help, but Cappy had shooed her away, saying she would put a nail through her finger.

Despite the freedom she had found on the bus, Kitty harbored a certain degree of homesickness and worry. But standing on that platform of plywood, shirt off, sinking nails with the sure strokes of a hammer, was someone who had touched a nerve she had never felt before. No way to compare Jubal with her fiancé: Victor was like egg custard and Key lime pie; Jubal made her want to pucker her lips, and made her tongue and throat tingle. Victor had never made her feel that way.

Early that morning on the parked bus, Kitty had rolled on her side and, half asleep, had realized her face was close to Jubal's. She had kept her eyes closed, felt his body against her skin. A shiver rolled down her spine when she sensed his lips against her forehead and the warm moisture of his tongue; she was surprised, but would not and could not withdraw. He moved his lips to a spot between her eyes, and she fairly hummed with pleasure. She was just tilting her face when Cappy, dozing in the driver's seat, farted so loud he woke himself. Jubal rolled away from her at once.

Kitty thought of the money in her pocket while she watched Jubal work. All she had were the couple of twenties Cappy had given her as pocket money after the last show. Fifteen hundred dollars: she had kept the show rolling. If she had to bail them out again, it would have to be with something other than money. The thought of being broke was frightening; Kitty suddenly felt small and alone.

THE LIVING ROOM of the ranch house was spacious, and its furnishings were rustic and plain. There were elk and caribou heads on the walls, a long gun case with at least a dozen firearms, and a large wood stove. Cappy and Virgil, sitting across from each other at a wooden table, were on their second glasses of whiskey. Virgil had already handed Cappy ten crisp hundred-dollar notes.

"Damn good scotch," Cappy said. "Ain't often I drink single-malt."

"I don't get it out much," Virgil replied. "But I like to enjoy myself when I do."

"You seem to have done well."

"I wasn't like most of those dopeheads in Hollywood. I saved and invested, and I still work six days a week."

Cappy nodded toward Virgil's shoulders. "What does your flag mean? I see it around here a lot."

Virgil set his glass down and pointed as he explained. "The red stands for all the blood the white man has shed to make this country what it is. The three X's are what we as white men must oppose to keep this country great: the federal government, capitalism, and integration. I'm sure you, as a southern man, agree."

Cappy drained his scotch, then set the glass down hard. "I agree some, although the federal government kept me fed and paid for thirty years. You know our dancer is black, don't you?"

Virgil nodded. "Jasper told me. I never said we were prejudiced. Any man of any color can join us. We can blend our politics, as long as we don't mix our blood."

"Thank you for your conversation and booze," Cappy said. "I better go on back. We have a show to do."

"Get the troops fired up. My boys are sure going to be."

Cappy nodded. The whiskey gnawed at his belly.

BY SEVEN O'CLOCK, the barn was full, with men mostly, all of them white and wearing the Freedom Ranch emblem on their shoulders. They drank beer from cans, and whiskey straight from the bottle. Many of them had firearms on their hips. Jubal and Cappy looked through the curtain at the boisterous group.

"What do you make of them, Cappy? Some kind of club?"

"More like a militia. One of them nutty groups."

"Then they ought to be into snakes and naked women."

"Certain women. I have a bad feeling about this place. We can't fight our way out of here."

Cappy decided to start the show with Jubal, to get the crowd heated up before Glory came out. He gave the audience his usual spiel, then opened the curtain to reveal Jubal poised with the big western diamondback curled up before him. Earlier that day, he had force-fed it three chicken franks, so that now, belly full, it was sluggish. Still, the snake struck three times before Jubal was able to snare it. After holding the serpent aloft, he bit the snake's rattle off with his teeth, then spit it into the crowd. Several men scrambled for the prize, one finally wielding it in triumph. Biting the rattle off looked impressive, but it didn't hurt the snake; Jubal knew it was made of dead tissue. If these men wanted to think better of him for biting it off, fine with him. He milked the snake's venom into a clear plastic cup, then drank the fluid. Some of the men moaned in disgust, others laughed and shouted encouragement.

"We ought to make him an honorary member," one of the men yelled.

"Bring on the tits," shouted another.

Glory, in a southern belle getup complete with blond wig, was on next. The men stomped their feet. Kitty put on a tape, and the first notes of "The Battle of New Orleans" filled the barn. Cappy pulled the rope to open the curtain.

Glory's cancan, her first dance, was met with cheers and applause. But the approval did not last long. The men's smiles went flat, and their voices grew loud and hostile.

"What the fuck is this?" someone shouted.

Virgil, in the front row, raised his arm and snapped his hand like a salute. Immediately, the talking stopped. His face was set in a grim smile.

"Pigger nussy!" someone else called out.

Glory kept dancing, gyrating to the music, mouthing the words that told a story of men fighting tyranny. She stripped down to the gold chains she wore next to her skin, and hoots and cackles rose from the crowd, obscene and mean-spirited. Another song began, and Glory stepped from the stage to focus on Virgil, her eyes locked on his. She straddled his lap and thrust against him while running her fingers through his hair. He maintained his tight smile while the catcalls mounted. Glory kissed his forehead, then slid her hands down his chest and across his crotch while backing off. She spun on the toes of one foot, a tornado of gold and black.

Faster and faster she twirled, until a shower of sweat rained from her wet hair. Virgil lifted his hand to his mouth, then leaned and spit twice on the floor. He narrowed his eyes, and stood and grabbed Glory's arm to bring her to a halt.

"You can fondle my dick, but I'm not drinking your sweat," he said. "Get your black ass back on that stage."

"Get the nigger out of here," a man shouted.

Glory stared at Virgil, then returned to the stage. She hesitantly resumed dancing, until a beer can came sailing out of the audience and skittered across the stage close to her feet.

Virgil spit on the floor again. "Cut the damn music," he shouted.

Cappy signaled to Kitty to stop the tape. Glory stood erect, her eyes wide with shock, as Cappy came to her side.

"You got a problem?" Cappy asked Virgil.

"You damn right I do." Virgil pointed at his shoulder. "Didn't I say one of those X's up there is against integration?"

"I ain't asking you to marry her, just watch her dance."

"I'll watch her dance, but I don't want her touching me."

A sob burst from Glory's mouth. She opened her mouth to speak, then turned and rushed off the stage. Kitty closed the curtain.

"Give me back my money, and get off my ranch. I paid you for a show."

"I'll give you half of it back. You saw half the show."

"I'm a fair man. Give me five hundred back, and hit the road."

"What war did you fight in, son?" Cappy asked. "What branch of the service did you serve in?"

Virgil stared at Cappy. "I'm fighting a war right now. All of us are."

"Tell you what. You're a big man, but I'll fistfight you for that other five hundred. Me and you, one on one."

Behind the stage, Kitty watched Glory hug Darlene and cry. Jubal walked onstage and stood beside Cappy. Kitty's ears were ringing, and tears welled in her eyes as she listened to Cappy. Deliberately, she changed the cassette tape, then pushed the play button and turned the volume all the way up. "Start Me Up" by the Rolling Stones. She had heard this before.

She didn't have Glory's moves or body, but when Kitty came through that canvas, she had been reborn. She motioned for Cappy and Jubal to get off the stage; they were so stunned they didn't argue. Mimicking Glory the best she could, Kitty stared above the audience and let the music take over. She felt detached from her body, as if she were floating above herself, watching herself rotate her hips and unbutton her blouse.

A murmur rolled through the crowd; then a few men began to cheer. Button by button, the garment came off, and the cheers grew louder. Kitty twirled to the music, remembering the dance classes she had taken as a girl. The blouse fell to the floor. Next the jeans. She was suddenly in a world of her own, in front of all these people. Her back to the audience, she reached behind and unhooked her bra. She turned around and let it fall to the floor.

She felt as if she was stepping through a door that for years had been locked tight. She heard only the music, and moved her body to a voice that spoke to her for the first time. She was made of light, wind. She was the only living soul on the face of the earth.

KITTY DANCED to three songs before she came off the stage. The bus was back on the road two hours later, Jubal at the wheel, Cappy holding the full thousand dollars.

Glory sat beside Kitty with her arms around her and whispered in her ear. "It's all right, honey. You did so fine. Them men didn't buy you. You had your price, and they paid it, and the trade was fair. You hear me? All they saw was a magic show. What you wanted them to see. The real Kitty is inside, still clean and pure."

They stopped at a state park for the night. No one said much over a late supper. While the others were still eating, Kitty excused herself. She took a quilt and went to sit in the darkness beneath the trees.

Jubal could barely see her form in the night.

"I reckon I'm gonna turn in," Cappy announced. "The show is over and done with, thank God. Next stop is Oregon."

Jubal waited a few more minutes before he got up from the table. He called to Kitty when he was several steps away.

"Can I talk to you?"

"Sure."

She hugged her knees with her arms. Jubal stood above her.

"I admire you," he said. "I more than admire you."

"Remember when you helped the corn snake shed its skin?" Kitty said softly.

"Yeah, I remember."

"Remember how sleek and pretty it was? The colors were so bright."

"I remember."

"I feel that way now."

Jubal knelt in front of Kitty. "I didn't look at you. I had my back turned the whole time."

Kitty smiled. A tear slid down one cheek. She got on her own knees facing Jubal, only inches from him. Without a word, she unbuttoned his shirt, then unbuttoned her own and pressed her breasts against his chest. Then she touched her lips to his.

THE BUS ROLLED farther westward, crossing mountains and descending into valleys, passing through desert and forest, and forgotten small towns and cities. They stopped only for food, gas, and bathroom calls; a sense of urgency was pushing everyone.

The bus was pulling out of a McDonald's when Jubal turned too sharply and ran over the curb. Just one of a thousand jolts that had rocked the bus in these many miles; the shocks creaked, and Cappy's beer toppled from where he had set it atop one of the coolers.

At the jolt, Darlene felt no pain, but the light in her eyes went out, as though someone had turned a switch. Where an instant before she was watching people and cars through the window, suddenly she saw only sparks of color, like particles of a bright rainbow sprinkled against a midnight sky. She said nothing for minutes, just clutched the magazine she had been reading and slowly tightened the pages into a roll. Finally she called to Cappy.

"Help me back to my bed. I think I'll lie down for a while."

"You feeling all right? You haven't eaten your burger."

"I'll eat it later. I want to rest for a while."

Even thicker than the darkness that had engulfed her was the weariness she felt, as if the very marrow of her bones had been sucked dry. She waited for Cappy's hand before she attempted to rise, and put most of her weight on him as he helped her to bed. She lay on her back.

"Close the curtain," she said softly.

"What's wrong, Darlene? You're pale as a ghost."

She patted the mattress beside her. "Sit down here." She reached with both arms and traced her hands across Cappy's brow, nose, and lips. "I'm blind."

Cappy tried to stand, but she held his arm. "Sit here awhile. There's no reason to hurry."

"We need to get you to a hospital. I'll tell . . ."

Darlene put her fingers to Cappy's mouth. "Hush." She stroked his face. "Clinton, we've been some miles together, haven't we?"

"I'd say a few."

"Take me on a few more. Take me to my land. Promise me this. Don't take me to a hospital. We knew this was going to happen sooner or later. Promise me."

"If that's what you want."

"Promise me."

"I promise."

She felt wetness on Cappy's cheeks, and wiped it away with her fingertips. "The first time in my life I've ever known you to cry, and I can't even see it."

A sob burst from Cappy's mouth. He leaned over and put his head beside hers. "Don't die on me, Darlene. You're the only thing in this whole goddamn world that ever meant anything to me." His shoulders heaved as he sobbed again.

"I'm right here, baby," she whispered. "I'm not going anyplace yet. You've got to let it go. Whatever it is you've been toting all these years, you have to let go."

Cappy held tight to Darlene as the bus rocked its way to the promised land.

THE MAN BEHIND THE DESK at the tax office in Bayview studied the deed that Cappy had handed him. He searched for Darlene's name in a thick book.

"Yeah, here it is. Ten point seven acres. Olympic Land and Realty Company."

"How come there wasn't no listing for the realty company in the phone book? I asked three people in town, and they hadn't ever heard of it."

The man thumped his pencil against his desk. "Sir, the man who operated this business only needed a post office box. But she does own the land. Legal and fair. She also owes about two thousand dollars in back taxes."

"How the hell does she owe that?"

"The same reason that the man she bought the land from is serving five to seven years right now. I wouldn't be so familiar with his case, except that about ten of his clients have been to see me in the past few years."

"What are you saying?" Jubal asked.

The man walked to a file cabinet. He pulled out a sheet of paper from a folder. "Here's your friend's land." A topographical map was marked with orange pencil. "One thing's for sure, she has a heck of a view."

CAPPY WENT to tell Darlene that the long journey had finally ended. He decided they should stock up on more food before continuing down the coast, and sent Kitty and Glory with Jubal to a supermarket.

Before entering the store, Jubal excused himself to find a rest room. He looked instead for a pay phone. He took a scrap of paper from his wallet, then dialed the operator.

"How can I help you?"

"Ma'am, I'd like to place a collect call to Los Angeles."

"What is the number you wish to call?"

Jubal read out the number.

"What is the name of the party you wish to speak with?"

"Jasper Dupree."

THE SPIT OF ROCK rose steeply and jutted out at an angle, a narrow wedge of granite with sheer cliffs that dropped nearly two hundred feet on each side. The western cliff fell to glistening black rocks, where the Pacific surf crashed into spray and foam. The eastern cliff was just as sheer, but at the bottom was a small lagoon, deep and blue, the water rising and falling only a few feet with the tides.

"So this is it?" Jubal asked.

"Hell, yeah."

"Nothing but a cliff?"

"Mostly. I wish I had my hands around that realtor's throat. She's got ten acres, but it's vertical."

"How are we going to tell her that?"

"We ain't."

THE BREEZE OFF THE OCEAN was rich: gulls wheeled and called in the thermals above the cliffs. Glory held one of Darlene's arms, Cappy the other.

"You smell that air?" Cappy asked.

Darlene breathed in deeply. "I smell it. Smells just like when I was a girl. Sea gulls. I can feel the sun on my face too. It's over there above the horizon, getting ready to sink into the water and lay a red carpet down on the ocean."

Cappy turned Darlene from the water. "You have a beautiful piece of land, Darlene. About eight acres of it is covered with juniper. Big, old trees. But there's a little clearing where we could build a house. Out the back window, you could see the sunset every evening."

"I won't need a house."

Cappy ignored her comment. "I can get me a skiff and learn to fish for lobster. There's money in lobster."

"I'm going to hire on a trawler," Jubal said. "I hear you can make twenty bucks an hour out here pulling nets."

"There's a slew of restaurants in town," Glory volunteered. "I'll get a job tomorrow and start saving some money. Couple months from now, I'll go ahead and open that beauty salon. I already got a name—the Dixie Do. Ladies be coming in wanting to look like Dolly Parton."

Darlene smiled sadly. "No. This is not your home. You'd never be happy here for long. Can't you look at yourselves? How do you think we made it all the way across the country? You're of a unique species and region. The rest of the country ridicules you. You need to walk your own path and keep walking. The sun will rise to your back and the land you see in front of you will be the home you left, and the home you have to return to. Just like I did."

Darlene's knees buckled. Cappy dipped and lifted her and carried her to the bus.

ON A ROCK above the sea, Kitty sat gazing at the crashing water. I'm at the end of the world, she thought, the end of the road. But not really. If I turn around, I'm right at the beginning.

Back in Wilmington, she remembered, she had gone into a Starbucks and phoned for a taxi, after a night in a cheap motel. Waiting at the curb outside, she played with a skinny kitten. She saw the bus pull into the service station across the street, read "Jubilee Express" on the side, watched Jubal get off and arrange boxes in the storage compartment, then fill the gas tank and enter the store. A police car turned the corner and passed her; the brake lights flared. When the car began backing up, she ran, then tripped in the middle of the street and dropped her purse. An officer stepped from the car and called to her. She ran behind the bus and crawled deep into the beckoning mouth of the storage compartment. When she was closed in utter blackness, she said the words "Jubilee Express" over and over. She remembered ordering the cappuccino at Starbucks, petting the frayed kitten. Her world had turned around in an instant. Goodbye, Cornelia Monroe, she told herself. Kitty Buckstar has been swept up by a chariot bound for some far land of joy.

The soothing pulse of the surf reminded Kitty how she felt when she and Jubal were intertwined. She imagined herself at her wedding, a wedding she would want, barefoot and in a long simple dress, with the harmonious winds and tides instead of a mournful

organ as accompaniment. She was even more glad now that she had
run from the altar back home.

I N   A   D R E S S I N G   R O O M in the rear of the church, where she
waited with Esther, Cornelia could hear the notes from the organ.
Soon the bridesmaids and ushers would enter, and then it would be
time for her to walk down the aisle on her stepfather's arm. Her
stomach twisted and churned.

"I'm sorry, Esther. I know you wanted to sit down front."

"I want to be right where you need me, honey. Another few
minutes, this will be all over."

The past week had been particularly bad. A tornado had passed
over Orton Plantation, where she had planned to be married in the
rose garden. The ceremony had to be changed to the church. Her
mother had been frantic all week with the rearrangements, and she
and Cornelia had hardly exchanged a civil word. Victor had been
working extra hours to cover the two weeks he was taking off for
the honeymoon, and they had seen each other only intermittently
and briefly. And now, after the argument she had had with him this
morning, she wondered whether she wanted to see him at all.

The rehearsal and dinner afterward had gone well the night before, and Cornelia had slept well, after taking a Valium. For a
brunch before the ceremony, she had put on a sundress that Victor
liked. The formalities were almost over, and in twenty-four hours
she and her new husband would be in Paris. Cornelia looked out a
window of her room, and was curious to see Victor sitting with her
stepfather at a table on the patio. The guests weren't due for another

hour. She quickly put on her makeup and returned to the window to make sure the two men had not left; she wanted to go downstairs and surprise them.

They were still at the table, bent over what looked like a map. Frank gestured as he talked, and pointed repeatedly at the map. He seemed to smile at Victor, who nodded very seriously. Cornelia instantly felt ice in her belly.

She hurried downstairs. As she approached the table, Frank folded the map. He stood and kissed her cheek. "Hello, dear. You look beautiful. I'll let you lovebirds be alone." He nodded sharply at Victor, and turned and walked away.

"You do look beautiful, Cornelia," Victor said. "I'll ask Esther to bring us some coffee."

"I don't want any coffee. What were you and Frank discussing?"

"Oh, just things. It's a big day, you know."

"What sort of things? Last night you didn't tell me you were coming early."

"I just thought I'd pop by before all the people get here. Discuss a few little business matters."

"Nothing in particular, Victor?"

"Look, why all the interest suddenly? Hey, I want some coffee. I'll be right back."

Cornelia knew she was being ignored, if not lied to. Her inheriting Boar Island was, to put it mildly, a sore spot for the family. She knew that her mother, fully expecting the property to come to her, had been furious after the reading of the will. Cornelia had heard through a friend at Hollins whose father handled the Monroes' legal affairs that the will had been challenged but was found to be iron-clad. She and her mother had never discussed the matter; in this family, you did not argue or even raise your voice with a family member, but simply had another drink or scheduled another visit with your therapist.

Victor returned carrying a tray laden with two cups and a pot of coffee. "I brought you a cup, anyway," he said. He set the tray down, then leaned and kissed Cornelia on the cheek. "This is a perfect day for a wedding. Aren't you excited?"

Cornelia took a deep breath and made herself speak. "Victor, why were you and Frank discussing Boar Island?"

Victor glanced quickly at Cornelia, then busied himself pouring coffee. "How did you know we were talking about Boar Island?"

"I saw you from the window. I saw you had a map. I figured that's what it was."

Victor swept back his perfect hair with his hand. "We were just talking real estate and development. That's our job."

"Not real estate and development on Boar Island. You know we've discussed that, Victor. I intend to leave the island just as Dad wanted it."

"That seems a little like spying, Cornelia. Watching us from your window, wondering what we're talking about."

"I wouldn't think my own stepfather and fiancé would have anything to hide from me on my wedding day."

Victor sipped his coffee. He smiled and stood. "Look, honey. I know you've been real tense this week. We all have. I'm not going to argue with you on such a special day. We'll both feel lots better tomorrow."

Ceremoniously, he stooped and kissed her again, then went in the house. Soon afterward, guests began to arrive, and Cornelia was once more the perfect bride-to-be and daughter.

CORNELIA'S WATCH read ten past five. She heard her roommate from Hollins begin singing in the chapel. Cornelia took a deep breath. When this song ended, there would be another, and then the prelude to the wedding march, and her stepfather would come to lead her away.

Her stomach twisted, and she put her hand to her mouth. "I can't do this, Esther."

"You can do it if you want to. But you got to want to." Esther grasped Cornelia's shoulder and turned her so they were face to face. "Do you want to marry that man, sugar? If you want to marry him, this ought to be a moment of joy for you."

"I *have* to marry him, Esther. Mother and Frank have done so much for me. I think I want to marry him. Mother says we're a good match."

Esther shook Cornelia hard. "You listen to me, child. Your mama and stepdaddy think of money like it's the angels of the Lord. Anything they need fixed or healed or removed from sight, they can write a check and it is done, like salvation from heaven. Victor, he's just the same. But he can't buy your heart. Can't nobody buy you love. Not real love. You got to know it's right before you marry a man."

"What would you rather be, Esther, rich or in love?"

"I'd rather be both, but I ain't rich. Never will be. I know this.

When I married my husband, I was dancing down the aisle. I was walking on air. That's what I want for you, honey. I want you dancing with joy when you marry the man you love."

Cornelia took a deep breath. "Esther, I would like to be alone for a few minutes. Frank will be here soon."

Esther pinched her cheek. "I'll be right outside."

Cornelia closed the door, then locked it. She stepped out of her gown and changed into the jeans she'd arrived in. She scribbled a note and laid it on the vanity, and patted one of her jeans pockets for reassurance. She had hidden a tote bag filled with extra clothes in the bushes outside.

Esther knocked on the door. "You okay, Cornelia?"

"I'll keep in touch, Esther." Cornelia walked to the window and opened it, then kicked the screen out and stepped through. As she ran across the church grounds, she felt a strength in her legs that she'd never felt before.

KITTY WAS PULLED out of her thoughts abruptly.

Glory was calling her. "Miss Darlene wants to talk with you."

Kitty lingered on the rock a few minutes more before going into the bus.

"You asked for me, Miss Darlene?" she asked from the doorway.

"Yes, honey. Come on in. Close the curtain behind you."

Kitty had butterflies in her stomach. As much as she admired the woman's grit, she was a little afraid of her.

"Sit here on the edge of the bed, please."

Kitty sat down gently, clasping her hands in her lap.

Darlene lifted her hand. Kitty froze as the woman placed it on her face and outlined her jawbone with her fingertips.

"This has been quite an adventure for you, hasn't it, Miss Monroe?"

Kitty's heart pounded. She tried to speak, but could find no words. Darlene lowered her hand.

"I knew your father way back when he fished with Jubal's daddy. He used to come into the bar down on Water Street. He was such a handsome man. You got his very same jaw.

"He used to brag on you, Cornelia. You were the center of his world. The name is Cornelia, isn't it?"

"Yes. How did you know who I was?"

"I wasn't sure at first. But I noticed a resemblance. I knew those hands of yours, well manicured, belonged to someone who'd grown up comfortable. I noticed your manners, and how you seemed to know more than the high school graduate you said you were. Then you found the money at the truck stop. Got the Captain out of jail. Went to the rest room and suddenly a hundred-dollar transmission appeared."

"I just wanted to help. That was the only way I knew."

"I was wary of you at first. Just a little rich girl rebelling, who would call Mama and fly home when things really got rough."

"I . . . I . . ."

"But you proved yourself when you went up on that stage. That wasn't money, Kitty, that was your heart that took you up there. I knew you were one of us then."

Tears dripped down Kitty's face. "Miss Darlene, in two days I turn twenty-one. I have an inheritance. A large one. I can get you in a hospital. The best one in Oregon."

"Shhhh. I don't want a hospital. I've lived my life, and it's been a good one. But there is one thing I want you to do for me."

"Name it."

"Clinton and Jubal both have a demon they're carrying that money will never cure. Only they can kill it. You've got to let this journey come to a head. You've got to let the cards fall and not interfere."

"I love Jubal. Cappy, he's a hero."

"I know. You've got a big heart, honey, just like your daddy. But money won't help Cappy and Jubal. They've got to quit running from their demons and face them."

Kitty held back her tears. "I won't interfere, Miss Darlene. I promise."

"Cornelia Monroe is a proud name to bear when it reflects her father. But Kitty Buckstar is a fine, brave young woman too. Can you be Kitty for a few more days?"

"I'll always be more Kitty than Cornelia, Miss Darlene. But I know that's all right now. All these miles it took me to finally look at myself."

"You only had to stop believing the illusion, Cornelia. You had to stop being the spectator and step up on the stage. You can't be passive in this world. Basically honest, and on fire with life. That's your heritage, honey."

"I know who I am now, and I know what I want, Miss Darlene. Finally I do. But for today and tomorrow, or however long it's necessary, I'm Kitty Buckstar."

Darlene patted Kitty on the arm. "Get the rest of them in here. Me and the Captain are finally going to be honest."

THE SMALL BEDROOM in the bus was crowded, but everyone managed to jam inside. Cappy wore a clean white shirt. He handed Darlene a bouquet of cut flowers. Jubal held two gold wedding bands bought at a pawnshop. Glory wore her best red dress, with wild flowers she had picked along the cliffs in her hair. In one hand she held a certificate from Blood of the Lamb Bible College. A few years back, she had purchased the mail-order document for twenty-five dollars; by decree of the college, she was a bona fide minister.

"I told you I wasn't lying, Jubal." Glory waved the paper in the air. "Billy Graham ain't got nothing on me. Now let's get started with this thing before we smother in here."

Cappy and Darlene clasped hands, and Glory raised her chin. "Now, I don't know the exact words to this, but I got the paper that says I'm a minister. This is the real thing. Cappy, you and Miss Darlene been knowing each other for a long time, and I know you love each other. It's in your eyes. I don't know why y'all didn't do this years ago. 'Cept for ol' goat-headed Cappy."

"This is a wedding, not a sermon," Cappy said.

"And you ain't supposed to talk back to the preacher. As I was saying, you two love each other, and now you want to be man and wife. Clinton Tucker, do you love Miss Darlene?"

Cappy nodded.

"I asked do you love her?"

"I nodded my head."

"Say the damn words!"

"I love her," Cappy growled.

"And Miss Darlene, do you love this thick-tongued—do you love Cappy?"

"Yes, I do."

"Let's get it on, then." Glory turned to Jubal. "Hand them the rings."

Jubal handed each a band.

"Now put the rings on each other's fingers."

Cappy's band was a little tight, but he managed to work it over the joint. Darlene's band fit perfectly. She touched her face with it.

"All right, by the power invested for twenty-five dollars, I announce you man and wife. You can kiss the bride."

Cappy stared at Glory.

"Kiss her. It ain't official till you kiss her."

Cappy pressed his lips to Darlene's. Glory, Jubal, and Kitty burst into applause.

"We have cake and champagne," Kitty said. "I'll get Miss Darlene the first helping."

Glory blew her nose into a tissue. Jubal patted Cappy on the back and pumped his arm up and down.

LATER THAT NIGHT, Jubal and Kitty made their bed above the cliffs, where they could hear the surf. Glory said she too would sleep outside, near the fire, so the honeymooners could have their privacy.

"Come on to bed," Darlene finally said after Cappy had lingered for an hour over a magazine. "I'm not going to bite you."

Cappy turned the lamps off, then undressed in the white light of the moon shining through the window. He lay down and after a few moments felt Darlene's hands on his chest and in his hair. Twice, she kissed his cheek.

"You know, we have to consummate the marriage," she told him.

"We can't do that," Cappy answered. "That piece of glass—I might hurt you."

"You'll hurt me a lot worse if we don't."

"I can't, Darlene."

"There never was any bullshit between us, Clinton, and it shouldn't start now. You know the score. I might have a day or two at most. You always did what you had to do, Clinton. Do it one last time."

He kissed her eyelids first, then her nose and mouth. He moved his lips gently, slowly, and a shiver crossed her shoulders. He'd always been that way in bed, nothing like the brawler he was in the rest of life. Darlene could feel his stubble of whiskers, the smell of frosting on his breath.

Time reversed, and Darlene was once again a long-legged dancer, Cappy a handsome soldier in uniform, his hair thick and black.

THE SPASM was pure white light and joy. It began minute, in the centermost cell of her brain, and within seconds was larger than the sun. It rolled down her spine, then raced back to her brain, exploding as pleasure and pain. She and the light became one, and as the light slowly faded, so did Darlene.

CAPPY CAST THE BOUQUET into the wind. The flowers tumbled end over end before hitting the water. The next wave buried them as it crashed against the rocks; the receding water sucked the bouquet into deeper surf, a bright spot of color against gray water.

"We brought her home," Cappy said, his face the same color as the sea. "She got her wish."

Glory blew her nose. She had been weeping most of the day.

As the flowers were swept seaward, a low afternoon sun broke through the clouds. A path shimmered across the water.

Earlier that morning, they had driven Darlene's body to the town morgue. After the coroner had decided her death was from natural causes, Cappy had given the mortician the few hundred dollars he had left as a deposit against her burial.

Cappy stared at the light on the water. "She's going to be above-ground. As long as this rock stands, she'll be able to look out toward the horizon."

"We can do another show," Kitty said. "You've got two dancers now. We'll raise twice the money."

"No." Cappy shook his head. "The show is over. Forever. My retirement check comes next week. I'll pay for the tomb. Get y'all back home."

"You've got to get home too," Kitty said.

Cappy didn't speak, just shook his head again.

"I've already got the matter taken care of," Jubal said.

Cappy stared at him. "How?"

"Back last week when things were looking tough, I called Jasper. He offered me a deal, and I called yesterday to accept it. He's sending up a private jet tonight to fly me and Glory down to Los Angeles."

Jubal looked at Kitty. "I'm sorry. I should have told you."

"Los Angeles?" Cappy exclaimed. "For God knows what?"

"For five thousand dollars. That's what. He's getting married again and wants me and Glory to do his bachelor party."

"Hell, no! Hell, no! Hell, no! I said the show is over."

"I'm going, Cap. The party starts at midnight tonight. That's too much money to turn down. We can bury Miss Darlene proper, and still have money to get home."

Glory nodded.

"Why is he paying five thousand dollars?"

Jubal hunched one shoulder. "Special party."

Glory broke her silence. "'Cause it's a king cobra. I tried to talk him out of going, but he's going, and I ain't letting him go alone."

"A king cobra! Son, are you nuts? It'll be the last show, all right, because when that thing bites you, you're a dead man."

"It's just another snake."

"No it ain't." Cappy stepped closer to Jubal. "It ain't even a snake. When you going to let Andy's death go? When you going to stop punishing yourself?"

"It's not Andy."

"He drowned, Jubal! But it wasn't your fault. You couldn't hold up a thousand pounds."

Jubal's eyes were shiny. He sucked in a quick breath. "You wouldn't have let go. If that had been your brother, you'd have hung on even if you were drowning too. You'd have jumped in after him."

Cappy opened his mouth, but the words were locked too deeply inside. He turned from Jubal and looked over the cliffs at the dark rocks below.

THE SMALL JET touched down on the runway, then taxied toward the terminal, where Glory, Jubal, and Kitty were standing.

"Don't do this, Jubal. We'll get the money somehow." Kitty wanted so badly to tell him and Glory that the next day she would be twenty-one, that with a simple phone call she could beckon her own jet like a legion of angels, but her promise to Darlene stood in the way. She also knew Darlene was right.

"Don't worry," Jubal reassured her. "Cobras aren't fast. Rattlers are a lot faster."

Kitty turned to Glory. "You know what they're going to want from you. It's a bachelor party."

"It won't be the first time, Kitty, but it *will* be the last. I'm going home, get my beautician license. I promised Miss Darlene that I would."

The jet had stopped and a door was opening. Jubal pulled Kitty to his chest. "You know I sort of love you."

"I love you too." Kitty laid her head against him and grasped his arms. "Jubal, that island you talked about. Boar Island. Anything is possible if you want it enough. You've got to believe in yourself."

Jubal smiled. "First I've got to snag a king cobra." He kissed her forehead.

Glory hugged her. "You take care of the Cap. He's in some mighty big pain. We be back tomorrow morning."

At the doorway to the jet, Jubal turned and waved. Kitty pressed her palm against the glass.

THE MANSION stood on a hill overlooking the ocean. Every window in the place was ablaze with light. Blue bulbs lit the paved driveway. Jubal and Glory sat in the rear seat of a limousine, gaping at the extravagance.

"Ol' Jasper must make some kind of money," Glory said.

"He's fixing to part with five thousand of it," Jubal answered.

Cars filled the grounds in front of the house: BMWs, Cadillacs, Mercedes-Benzes, Corvettes, all parked in neat rows by a valet. At the massive door to the house, Jasper, wearing only a black bikini, greeted Glory and Jubal.

"Damn glad to see you again." He gave each of them a big hug. In one of his hands was a bottle of champagne. "How's the Captain and Miss Darlene?"

"Miss Darlene died yesterday."

Jasper's smile did not falter. "We all have to go sometime."

He put an arm over Glory's shoulder and walked them both into the house. "Let me introduce you to the crowd."

A hundred men and women were assembled in a marble-floored ballroom. Some men were in tuxedos, some women in long evening dresses, but most people were casually attired, in jeans and bathing suits. They clustered in small groups, holding their drinks, talking and laughing. The air was blue with marijuana smoke. A band played loud rock-and-roll in one corner of the room. Against one wall was a generously stocked bar, and next to it, tables laden with food. In the center of the room was a smaller table, and on it a mirror, a mound of white powder, razor blades, and a rolled-up bill. A small stage covered with red velvet had been set up on one side of the room. On it sat a large glass cage with a coiled nine-foot king cobra inside. A brass padlock secured the door.

Glory raised an eyebrow at Jubal. "We in the den of iniquity," she whispered.

Jubal was already reading the snake, its olive skin, its scales etched with black, its pale blue eyes.

Jasper ushered them to the stage and motioned for the band to stop playing. He waved his arms and whistled until silence fell over the room.

"Friends, I have a special attraction for you tonight. I want to introduce Gloria Peacock and Jubal Lee. They came all the way from the South to do a special show." Jasper put his arm around Glory again. "Gloria here, well, you'll just have to see her with your own eyes. And Jubal"—Jasper pointed at the cobra—"he's going to catch that cobra with his bare hands, and when he does, everyone in here is going to have to change their shorts."

The people applauded briefly, then returned to their merriment. A line had formed at the cocaine table, as one man cut several fat lines from the mound. A blonde woman in a red bikini bottom and lacy white bra emerged from the crowd; she smiled and waved toward the stage.

Jubal recognized her immediately as the woman who had been with Jasper that last time at The House of Joy, the one who had gotten drunk and climbed onstage to dance.

"That's my bride," Jasper said, waving to the woman. He then led Jubal and Glory to a bedroom. On the vanity was a tray of hors d'oeuvres and a fifth of scotch.

"Make yourselves at home. I'd like to start the show in about thirty minutes. If you want some dust, I'll bring you a bag."

Jubal shook his head.

Jasper held out an envelope. He counted out five thousand in hundred-dollar bills and slapped the bills against his palm. "This is a lot of money."

"I appreciate you being so generous," Jubal said. "We can sure use it."

"Never in my life did I think I'd get to ride in one of them little ol' jets," Glory said.

"Yeah, it's a lot of money, but a man doesn't get married for the fifth time every day." Jasper shifted his eyes from Glory to Jubal. "I expect you to earn it."

"I'll bust a gut dancing," Glory said.

"I have a few special favors to ask," Jasper said. "This being a special party."

"What?" Jubal asked.

"Glory, I want you to start off with a table dance for me and my ushers."

"I've done table dances."

"But when you finish, I want you to get under the table and give me and the boys a little something extra."

"Extra what?"

"You know what I mean, Glory. Don't embarrass me."

Glory's eyes narrowed.

"That wasn't in the deal," Jubal said.

"We're making a new deal. Now, for you, Jubal, I have a dandy. When you catch that cobra, I want you to slit its throat with your pocketknife and let the blood run in a goblet. Then I want you to drink it. I hear cobra blood is considered a mighty fine aphrodisiac. You're going to need it. Kelli wants an hour with you afterward."

For a moment Jubal was speechless. "I—I can't do that."

"Hell, no!" said Glory. "He ain't."

"Listen now, people." Jasper dragged out his words. "We're talking big money here."

"I'm not doing it," Jubal answered. "I'll catch the cobra and Glory will dance. That's what we agreed on."

"But we're reagreeing, son. Everybody has his price. Every man in the world."

"What if I do my part and Jubal just catches the snake?" Glory asked.

"Noooo. Kelli's been wanting Jubal since she first saw him."

"She's fixing to be your *wife!*" Glory exclaimed.

"It's a wedding present."

Jasper counted off bills until he held ten thousand dollars in his hand. "It's all or nothing. It's a long walk back to Oregon."

Jubal shook his head again. "That wasn't the deal, Jasper. I'll catch the snake and Glory will dance. That's all. You give us the money we agreed on, and we'll give you the show."

A smile spread over Jasper's face. "Son, you're in California now. Not the South. Things are different here."

"Where we come from, a man's word is his honor," Jubal answered. "That's the tradition. A lot of people don't have much more."

Jasper shook his head and his smile grew meaner. "Shit, Jubal. What are you talking about? What fucking honor? Glory's a whore and you're a freak. Tradition—shit! Down there you have grandsons selling off poor old hardworking Grandpa's land for cold cash. Wake up, son. There isn't a South any longer. It's just the good ol' United States of Assholes."

Jubal's face burned with anger, his mind whirling as he searched for words.

Jasper slapped the money against his palm again. He looked at Glory. "I'll change the deal. Glory, you do the table dance and the little extra for me and the boys, and John Boy can just catch the snake."

Glory nodded.

"Then afterward me and you and Kelli will go for a little romp. Kelli isn't real choosy."

Glory didn't speak. She held Jasper's stare.

"Ten thousand dollars. All or nothing." Jasper stuffed half of the money into Jubal's shirt pocket. "Just part of the tradition, Jubal. You southern gentlemen always let your niggers do the hard work, anyway. I'll call for you in about thirty minutes." He turned and left the room.

G LORY AND J UBAL hardly spoke during the time that passed. Glory's mind raced as she dressed.

Lord, I know it's a sin this time. A big sin. Always, in the past, I been doing the selling, but this time I'm being bought like a hog at market. And Jubal. He still clean. He still got a chance to get out of this life. But we need the money so bad. Miss Darlene gonna have a monument to the sky. Right up to the sky!

Jubal was on his second glass of whiskey when Glory came out of the bathroom.

"Put that stuff down," she told him. "Don't start taking Cappy's path."

"This is wrong, Glory. We've gone too far. We're human beings, not freaks."

"We're broke human beings. We got a dead woman to bury, and an orphan and a broken old man to feed. I can do my part. You just don't get bit by that snake."

Jasper tapped on the door and opened it. "Showtime." He smiled when he saw Glory in her costume.

"I'm not watching her under that table," Jubal said. "You come get me when you're ready to open the cage."

"Will do. This won't take too long. The boys are primed and ready."

Jubal heard the audience cheer as Glory went onstage. Music pumped from the band. A minute passed. Another. The roars from the audience continued. Jubal felt the money in his pocket. He stared into the mirror on the wall. Tears filled his eyes, and he felt as if he were staring upon water.

JUBAL LOOKED INTO HIS BROTHER'S EYES. The drone of the powerboat grew faint until all he could hear was the lap of the surf against the bulwarks. As the marlin settled lower into the depths, the pull on Jubal's arms strengthened steadily. He tore his eyes from his brother; the powerboat was now only a dot against the horizon. Jubal looked about wildly and saw no other vessel.

"I caught a hog, didn't I, little bro?" Andy said. He was smiling.

"I'm going to get you loose," Jubal said. "Keep holding to my arm."

Andy was underwater from the waist down. The sea turned pink around him; the fishing line was slicing into his leg. Andy closed his eyes. A gull called from above the boat.

"Keep your eyes open!" Jubal shouted. "Don't pass out."

Andy opened his eyes. "You're going to be the first Lee ever to get a college degree, Jubal. The very first."

Inch by inch, the weight of the great fish was pulling Andy farther underwater. Jubal jammed his foot between two struts and leaned back as far as he could. His hands began to slip. He searched the horizon again. A boat was coming in their direction; it was still more than a mile away.

"There's a boat coming, Andy. Just hang on. They'll see we're in trouble."

"A marine biologist," Andy said. "You can help save these waters. There's still time."

"Hush, Andy. Just be quiet and hold on to me. That boat will be here soon." Jubal looked behind himself. He could see the handle of a fillet knife in the tackle box. The water had turned bright red. Andy's fingers loosened.

"God damn it, don't give up!" Jubal screamed. "Hold on to me!" His shoulders burned like fire; his arms felt detached from the sockets.

"Promise me you'll finish. You got to. You always were the smartest one."

"Shut up!" Jubal was crying in rage. "You could have made the major leagues. Why in God's name did you quit!"

Andy's fingers relaxed, and his arm slid between Jubal's hands. Only his head and arm were above water. Jubal's fingers were numb. The approaching boat was larger now, but it seemed to have slowed, as if the fishermen were dropping lines. Tears dripped from Jubal's cheeks onto his brother's head.

"I didn't quit, Jubal. I flunked out. I was ashamed to say so."

"You *are* smart!"

Andy's arm slid between Jubal's fingers again until all he held was Andy's wrist. His chin was barely above the water. As he pulled his head back, he was smiling again. "I love you, brother."

"I love you too," Jubal whispered hoarsely.

Andy's hand slipped from Jubal's, and in an instant he was beneath the surface. Jubal whirled and grabbed the handle of the knife, then jumped off the stern. He dived until his lungs were filled with fire, but Andy steadily receded before him, his face white against the quickly gathering depths.

JUBAL REFOCUSED on the mirror. He stared deep into the reflection of his eyes.

Who will tell Andy's story if I don't? I can run from it, but he will always lie at the bottom of that water.

Carolina was meant for clean water and good fields, men and women drawing their life and livelihood from fishing nets and tobacco leaves. That's where the stories come from—not from condos and speedboats, but from people trying to make sense out of chaos, as Kitty tried to explain to that man in Colorado.

I am a part of the South, I know chaos and have had my hands in the flames. I have dreams and fears and hopes and promises, and if I must first labor in books before I can fill nets the way my brother and father did, I am no less a part of the breed. On my deathbed, I will judge myself more harshly for what I did not do when I was able than for what I tried to do and failed. I can grasp a rattlesnake in my hands and say, "Look at me. I am different. Expect less." I can grip that same snake and say, "I am different. Expect more."

Jubal wiped his tears with his hand. He could still hear the throb of the music and, above that, people cheering. Time to stop this shit, he thought. He gripped the whiskey bottle by the neck and flung it against the wall, where it shattered, brown streams of liquor coursing down like tiny rivers. He leaped toward the door.

When he entered the ballroom, Glory was still on the table. She could hardly dance because of the men grabbing her legs. One of the men was trying to get her to take a joint. People in the audience were laughing, their eyes wide, and red, and glazed.

"You fuckers want a show?" Jubal shouted. When he stepped onstage, Glory stopped dancing. They held each other's gaze for a moment.

Jasper stood up. "It ain't time for you!"

Jubal pulled at the padlock on the glass cage, but it was secure. The cobra rose from its coil and flared its hood four feet above the floor of the cage. Its eyes were a cold blue.

In a fluid motion, Jubal pulled his shirt over his head. He took the money from the pocket and threw it toward the crowd, then wound the shirt around his right hand. He reared toward the cage and slammed his fist into the glass. The cobra slid from the cage and rose again, facing him.

The music stopped; everyone in the audience froze in place. Jubal ripped his shirt from his hand. When the cobra lunged, he easily dodged the blow. The cobra rose once more. Jubal extended his left arm to one side, and the cobra's head followed; Jubal flashed with his right, snaring the snake just below the head. With his free hand, he grasped the snake's midsection and held on tightly. The cobra writhed and struggled, much stronger than any rattler Jubal had ever handled.

Jubal walked to the edge of the stage and motioned for Glory to get down from the table. She turned toward Jasper and kicked him in the chin.

"There's your blow job," she cried. In an instant she was off the table and standing beside Jubal.

He held the snake over his head and yelled: "Showtime!" He lunged forward as if he meant to throw the cobra on Jasper's table. "Here, Jasper, catch. You're the real freak."

The people at the table moved backward and screamed. Jubal bent down and put the snake on the stage; the cobra immediately rose into striking position.

Jasper's guests rushed from their seats, spilling their chairs, knocking into and tripping over one another. The cocaine mirror was in fragments on the floor, its contents dusting the carpet.

"Let's go!" Jubal pulled at Glory's arm. He picked up his shirt and some of the bills that had landed on the stage. They sprinted to retrieve the rest of their clothes, then exited at the rear of the house.

"Don't look back," Glory warned, "or you'll turn into a pillar of salt."

ON A BLANKET under a juniper tree, Kitty lay looking at patches of sky through the branches. She had a view of the road that led into town, and behind her the rock jutted out and up from the cliffs like a long finger pointing toward the heavens.

They should have been back already, she thought. Noon had long passed. She had woven a chain from clover blossoms and wore it around her neck. She was twenty-one years old. An official adult. A wealthy adult. And she felt like an adult, after what she had witnessed and experienced in the past few weeks. She knew now, as she had not known before, that happiness did not come from money in the bank, that when you were hungry, a can of Spam was as good as filet mignon. A million dollars would not equal a quarter to her until Jubal came down that road, his limbs and life intact.

She sat up and peered down the road. Nothing but a black stripe hugging the cliffs. She glanced toward the bus. Cappy had eaten no breakfast but had drunk beer after beer. At noon, when she had gone outside to wait for Jubal and Glory, Cappy was in Miss Darlene's room with the door closed. If Jubal and Glory hadn't returned by dusk, she would drive the bus into town and call Esther and tell her how she now stood on the edge of the world. She wished she could shout loud enough for Jubal to hear her, her voice a foghorn to guide him.

I AM A PERSON of the earth now, a human being. I am tied to a land and a time, and although I am not southern in the sense that Jubal and Glory and Cappy can claim that title, I am of the same species.

It's hard for me to believe that only weeks ago I often thought of death. Right now I am so full of life and potential that I could burst. If Jubal and Glory would just come around that curve, so I could run to them and tell them all the problems are over. I know I can't do that yet. Miss Darlene was wise.

In a way I feel like an angel, with the power to descend and carry us all back to North Carolina. Like the angels sent to Daniel in the lions' den or to the men cast into the fiery pit.

Until the day I entered the Jubilee Express, my body was as transparent as crystal, and as fragile. I was composed not of bone and muscle but of the invisible electricity of fears and the vapor of uncertainty. And everything I had been or was to be was bought and paid for; I had never worked a day in my life. I didn't know the good sweat of hard work, but tears were familiar. I cannot say that I have healed completely, but now I see my hands and arms and legs differently; my skin feels clear, touched by fresh air and sun.

Am I rich on paper this morning? A banker would say so. But

money possesses no divine spirit. I am far richer in what my heart holds; it is as large as Boar Island. I realize now why Cappy won medals, why Miss Darlene had to come home. Their ties to earth and heritage are like that gleam I saw in my father's eye when he asked that I bring my children to that beach one day and tell them I had stood with him on this spit of sand, as I did now with them, and ask only that they continue the tradition.

My blood is the flow of the river, my marrow the soil upon which generations have stood. On this day I could buy Jubal gold, but better, I could offer him my flesh and life and a taproot into a land he loves, a land he has tried to persuade himself to leave.

Slowly and deliberately Cappy shed his clothes and put his old uniform on. After all the years since retirement, his dress greens still fit. He pulled on his boots, laced them tight, and rubbed the leather with a rag until the shine appeared. He knotted his tie, then put on his jacket and secured the brass buttons; the left breast was brightened with the evidence of his many campaigns. Last he placed his beret on his head and cocked it at the proper angle. He lifted his arm in a smart salute.

Kitty walked to the roadside and sat on a tree stump to wait. Her heart beat faster each time a car or truck appeared, but each time the vehicle sped by with only a glance from the passengers.

She looked to the west to check the progress of the sun. A hundred yards away, also gazing toward the western horizon, was Cappy. He stood on a spine of rock overlooking the ocean.

What in the world was he doing? Kitty took several steps forward. When she saw him raise his arms into the air, she began running toward him.

"Captain!" she shouted. "What are you doing?"

He was still fifty yards away. He had stepped to the lip of the seaward cliff.

"What are you doing up there?"

"Stay down!" Cappy shouted.

Kitty ignored the sheer drop on either side and scrambled up the narrow spine of rock. She made her way until she was within thirty feet of Cappy. "What are you doing up here? Why are you wearing your uniform?"

"Because I'm going to jump." He still stared toward the horizon.

"Why do you want to do that? You'll kill yourself."

"That's the plan."

"Why do you want to kill yourself?"

Cappy lowered his arms. He turned his head and looked at Kitty. "Because Darlene is dead. Because Jubal probably is. Because I didn't jump once before, and men died. Why should I live?"

"Jubal and Glory are on their way back. You've got me. And I've got money, Cappy. I can take us all home."

Cappy shook his head. "I've been a coward all my life. Even if you had a million dollars, it wouldn't fix that. I've got to take that jump."

Kitty remembered Darlene's words. She understood then what demon it was that Cappy had to kill.

JUBAL, in the bed of the truck, tapped on the roof, and the pickup stopped. He and Glory stepped down, thanked the driver, and started toward the bus. They were nearly there when they noticed the two figures on the cliff.

"What in the world they doing up there?" Glory asked.

"I don't know," Jubal answered, "but it doesn't look good."

KITTY TOOK A FEW STEPS toward Cappy. He turned and pointed at her.

"Go back! I don't want you seeing this."

"You're not a coward, you're a hero. You won a Silver Star. You saved men's lives."

"And I took men's lives. I want you to turn around and walk down that rock."

Kitty heard Darlene speak to her then, as clearly as she had spoken from her bed days before.

Jump to the east, said the voice in her head. *The water is deep there. You can save him.*

Kitty looked at the cliff behind her, and the dark blue lagoon two hundred feet below. She stepped backward, then put her hand to her forehead.

"I feel dizzy, Cappy. I feel very dizzy." She stepped back again until her heels were on the edge of the rock.

"Sit down!" Cappy ordered.

Kitty raised both hands to her forehead and arched her back. She sensed a rush of wind, then flashes of sunlight and water.

CAPPY RAN to the spot where Kitty had gone over, saw her falling and falling and falling. She hit the water back first and went under.

"Oh, God. Oh, shit." He braced his legs to gather his strength, then leaped into the air. He moved his arms in circles to keep his feet down. His eyes were wide open when the water swallowed him.

JUBAL AND GLORY were almost to the base of the granite spine when Kitty fell. They watched her flight in horror, and seconds later saw Cappy jump.

"Please, God, no!" Jubal scrambled down the steep rock toward the lagoon. He reached the bottom, and stood on a sheer three-foot ledge above the water.

First Cappy's head appeared in the water. A moment later, Kitty's face emerged. Cappy was cradling her head under one arm, treading water and looking about desperately for a place to swim.

"Over here!" Jubal waved his arms. "Cappy. Over here!"

Glory had made her way to the lagoon. She stood by Jubal and joined him in yelling. Cappy tried to swim toward them, kicking at the water with his booted feet. Kitty, stunned, moved her legs weakly. They were at least a hundred feet from the ledge where Jubal and Glory stood.

Jubal kicked his shoes off and dived in. He raced to Cappy and Kitty. Cappy's face was bright red; he was breathing hard. Kitty's face was pale.

"'Bout damn time you got here." Cappy swore between breaths. With Kitty between them, Jubal and Cappy swam toward the ledge, where Glory was shouting encouragement. "You 'bout here. You 'bout here. Just a few more yards."

At the base of the ledge, the water was still heaving over their heads. Kitty was beginning to mumble.

"Just tread water," Jubal told her. "I'll get on the rock and pull you up."

Cappy gasped for air, his uniform and boots dragging him down. "You better hurry, boy."

Jubal grabbed the rock and hauled himself up. He lay on his stomach and extended his arms to grasp Kitty's wrists. Cappy still had her shoulders. He kicked the water with the last of his strength.

"Let her go, Cap, I got her now," Jubal said as Kitty gripped his wrists. He secured her over the lip of the rock, and Glory pulled her farther onto dry rock.

"Get him!" Glory shrieked. "He's going under!"

Turning to the water, Jubal saw only the top of Cappy's head. He leaned over the ledge until he could grab a handful of hair, and then drew Cappy's face above the surface. Cappy coughed and spewed water.

"Give me your hand."

Cappy raised his arm and Jubal clasped the man's wrist. "Hold on to me. I'm pulling you up."

Cappy could apply only slight pressure to Jubal's wrist. His eyes were glassy. "Just let me go, boy."

"No, dammit! Don't do this to me, Cap." A sob burst from his mouth. "I'm pulling you out, or I'm going with you."

Glory lay across Jubal's legs. "Y'all go, we all going."

Jubal gritted his teeth and began lifting. He rose higher and higher, until both of Cappy's elbows were over the ledge. Jubal's hand flashed from Cappy's wrist to his jacket collar. He roared as he expended the last of his strength. Cappy was up and over the ledge, and they both fell on dry ground.

FOUR FIGURES lay in a pile on the warm rocks for nearly an hour, alternately weeping and laughing and hugging. A gull flew in and watched them unobserved. When they regained enough strength to climb toward the bus, the gull spread its wings and disappeared above the cliff. A half-sun lay on the horizon.

THEY ATE DINNER, a tin of beef stew, in the glow of the lantern. "So you kicked ol' Jasper in the mouth," Cappy said. "I wish it could have been my fist."

"You should have seen those people running when Jubal turned that snake loose. I pity the poor ol' animal control man that had to come into that place."

Jubal scraped his plate with his fork. "I'm glad we got here when we did. You've always been my hero, Cap. You're like God now."

"Aw, don't say that. Kitty wouldn't have fell if my fool ass hadn't been on that cliff. You've got a grip there, Jubal. I was a goner. I was totally whipped. You gave me back my life, son."

Jubal smiled. "So what's the game plan? I have about a thousand dollars left of Jasper's money."

"Give it to Kitty," Glory said. "Knowing her, she can touch it and make two thousand appear, like Jesus and them fishes."

Cappy looked at the stars overhead. "I don't think it's up to me anymore to determine what we do. It's time to pass the torch."

"You ain't gonna climb that cliff again, are you?" Glory asked.

Cappy shook his head slowly. "No. I'm not going to kill myself. That's the easy way out. I realize that now. Living is a lot tougher."

"You got us to live for," Glory said. "We a family."

Cappy nodded. "My retirement check will be in my account tomorrow. I'll wire the bank and get money to bury Darlene and get us home."

Kitty had been eager to talk all night, to recount her story, to tell them that with a couple of days' legal work she could fly them all home on a Learjet. But the day had already carried enough drama, and she held her tongue. Still, the glow she felt inside was like the sunrise.

"What will you do when you get home, Cappy?" Kitty asked.

"I'm not sure. Maybe open me up a little bait-and-tackle shop where The House of Joy stood. Sell minnows and tell lies. I might promote myself to brigadier general."

Cappy reached into the cooler for a beer. "But I'm the past. I'm weary of fighting. It's you three that have to get busy. You're all still young, you have the world at your feet. We're going home, but home is changing, and for the worse, I think. You have a proud heritage, and you can't be the generation to lose it. The South has her problems, but God damn, she's clung together through it all. She's stood because of a mixture of people thrown in together with dirt under their fingernails and clay on their soles. The future ain't pretty little white subdivisions and black housing projects."

He took a long swallow of beer. "We're a mixed-up lot, but we made this trip because we cared about each other. We needed each other. You're going back to a place that's crumbling, and I don't have the answers. You've got to fix it. It might not be too late."

THAT NIGHT, Kitty and Jubal made their beds in a place where they could hear the surf, the surge and ebb of water like the pulse of time. Kitty lay with her face against Jubal's shoulder.

"Cap's right," Jubal said. "We've got to fix things. This last year, I've been running, but I'm going to turn and fight now. Me and you together, I feel like we can take over the world."

"What if I was rich, Jubal? What if I told you I was one of the Monroes, and I had money and could give you the title to Boar Island?"

Jubal chuckled. "I'd ask you to marry me. The war would be easier."

"And what if I'm only an orphan with a lot of dreams?"

"I'd ask you to marry me just as quick. I get rich either way."

Kitty snuggled tighter against him. "Are you asking?"

"Yes."

They listened in silence to the wind and surf.

"Are you accepting?" Jubal finally asked, his voice husky.

"Yes."

THE NEXT MORNING, the members of The Last Great Snake Show ate breakfast in town. Afterward they cleaned out the bus. Everything from the show was brought to a dump site, except the snakes; these would be returned to their swamps and meadows back home.

When they drove to town, Kitty asked to be dropped off near the post office. She went to a pay phone and dialed. Three rings, and she heard Esther's voice.

"Monroe residence."

"Esther, it's me."

"Lord God, thank you! Child, where are you? You have this house in an uproar. Your mother has the police looking for you."

"Shhhhh," Kitty said. "Just listen to me. I have a lot to tell you. But first I want you to do a big favor for me. Go to my bedroom closet, and get out my ballet shoes. I'm ready to dance now."

CAPPY LINGERED beside Darlene's tomb. He had told the others to board the bus.

I'm not leaving you for long, wife, he thought. One day, I'll be resting here right beside you. I'm not sure about a lot of life, but I do know it's a journey. You brought us here for a reason I understand now. It's time for me to take them home. Then the war is theirs.

Cappy took his wallet out of his pocket. From inside, he removed a folded plastic bag.

Darlene, this here is dirt I scooped from the yard in front of The House of Joy. It'll keep you company until they bring my bones back here.

Cappy knelt, then pressed his forehead against the cool stone.

JUBAL WATCHED the man approach the bus, his steps halting at first, then lengthening to a full stride. He climbed on the bus and took a seat beside Glory.

"Fire it up, boy. Let's go home."

Jubal smiled as he turned the ignition; the old motor roared to life.

"All right," he said to Kitty. "You've been saying you had something good to tell us, but we had to be on the road first. We've got a lot of miles of sitting. Why don't you begin?"

"God, Jubal. It'll take days for this story."

Jubal lifted one hand from the wheel and twisted it behind himself to hold her hand. "I hope I'll be listening to you for the rest of my life."

Kitty began slowly, a tale of two men who once fished the waters off an island in the mouth of the Cape Fear River. The bus receded from the coast, bound for the South, a spot of Carolina blue against the breast of America.